PHILIPPINES

PACIFIC OCEAN

Sulawesi

Moluccas

Irian Jaya

PAPUA
NEW
GUINEA

Tenggara

Roti

AUSTRALIA

THE MAGIC CROCODILE

AND OTHER FOLKTALES

FROM INDONESIA

The Magic Crocodile and Other Folktales from Indonesia

Told by
Alice M. Terada

Illustrations by Charlene K. Smoyer

A Kolowalu Book
University of Hawaii Press
Honolulu

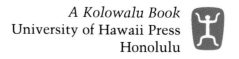

99 98 97 96 95 94   5 4 3 2 1

Library of Congress Cataloging-in-Publication Data

Terada, Alice M.
    The magic crocodile and other folktales from
Indonesia / told by Alice M. Terada.
        p.   c.m.
    Includes bibliographical references.
    Summary: An illustrated collection of twenty-nine
traditional tales from six regions of Indonesia.
    ISBN 0–8248–1654–4
    1. Tales—Indonesia. [1. Folklore--Indonesia.] I. Title.
PZ8.1.T259Mag   1994   94–10876
398.2'09598—dc20   CIP
                                              AC

Designed by Paula Newcomb

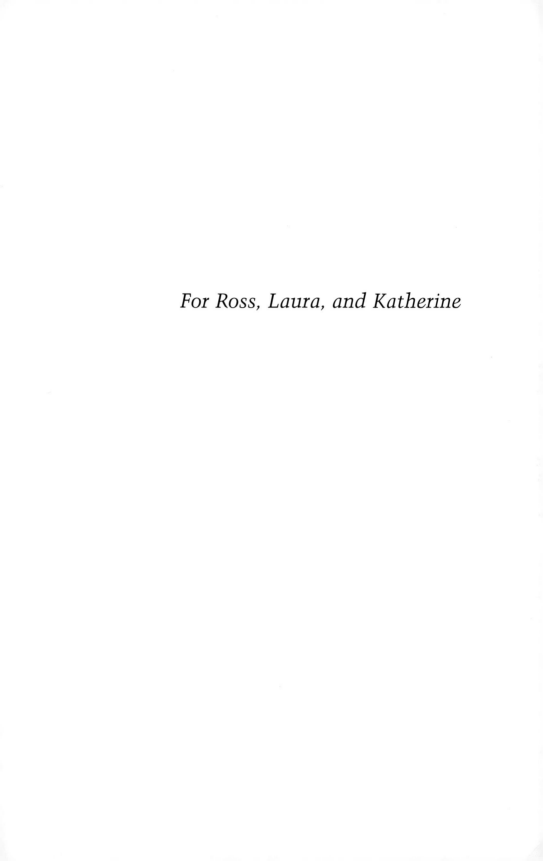

For Ross, Laura, and Katherine

Contents

Once, the Dayaks say, there was only sky and space. Not even earth or sea was there.

One day, a spider on its silken string dropped from the sky ever so slowly, spinning its web as it descended into the emptiness. It hung there, swinging, the only living thing in space. Then a red stone fell from the sky and was caught in the web. This red coral stone grew and spread until it filled the space beneath the sky and formed a mat like a floor.

Onto this red mat next tumbled a slug and a worm, whose bodies stuck to the mat and formed soil, which eventually covered it. And into this soil came a tree from heaven, with roots that went deep and brought forth other trees.

Next to drop from the sky was a crab, scampering over and into the soil, plowing rivers and heaping soil into peaks and valleys. Then came rain that filled the rivers and lakes and watered the earth so it could send forth rice and grass and weeds, and many other plants.

Finally, a male spirit and a female spirit dropped from the sky. They made their home under a tree where the man spirit made a wooden sword handle and the woman spirit made a loom. The sword handle fell and became tangled in the loom. After a period of time, the loom gave birth to one human head, followed by another.

The two heads married and produced two children, each with head and neck. These married and had two children, each with head and neck and rump. They married and, likewise, had two children, this time with head, neck, rump, and long arms that reached the sky. They were the gods of agriculture, Amei Awi and Burung Une. *

As the Dayaks of Borneo spin this tale, they explain how the earth was eventually peopled with humans.

With two to three hundred different language and cultural groups, each with its own myths and legends to tell, the islands of Indonesia are rich with stories. Included in these tales are themes and details that reach back almost two thousand years, stories that reflect the coming together of people from different nations and the introduction of the major religions of the world: Hinduism, Buddhism, Islam, and Christianity. In addition, slumbering volcanoes erupted through part of the island group. How frightened the people must have been when the earth trembled and exploded. One can only guess at which stories and beliefs were created to explain these volcanic events that occurred frequently over the centuries.

The stories in this book reveal the Indonesian islands from Sumatra in the west to Irian Jaya in the east. They were selected to give you an understanding of the Indonesian people through their myths, legends, and folktales. Notes that add background follow each story. These twenty-nine tales only scratch the surface of Indonesian folklore, but read them. Enjoy them. They are your introduction to Indonesia.

NOTE

*J. Knappert, "Myths and Legends of Indonesia," pp. 116–119.

Acknowledgments

I gratefully acknowledge the invaluable services of Enny Riningsih Soekarman Williams in translating, interpreting Indonesian customs and beliefs, and explaining traditions. Sumastuti Sumukti ensured the accuracy of facts and traditional beliefs. I appreciate the scholarship she has brought to this collection. To Norma Gorst, editor, poet, and writer, I extend my gratitude for reading and editing my drafts. Finally, I thank Iris Wiley, executive editor of the University of Hawaii Press, for the support she has given me from the very beginning.

Indonesia

The archipelago of Indonesia (see endpapers) consists of 13,677 islands and includes the better part of three of the six largest islands on Earth: New Guinea, Borneo, and Sumatra. The Indonesian portion of Borneo is known as Kalimantan. The western half of the island of New Guinea is Indonesian and is known as Irian Jaya. The entire island of Sumatra is Indonesian.

Sumatra

One Sun

WHEN the great god Mulojadi saw how wet the newly created earth was, he made nine suns to dry the earth. The earth became drier, and in a few short years, it became parched.

Creatures on earth suffered through the heat of each day. Only night brought relief. One evening, after the heat had been more intense than usual, the people gathered on an open plain to pray to the moon. The moon rose in full splendor.

"Oh, Moon, please help us," they pleaded. "The searing heat of the suns is too much for us."

"I have no power to fight the suns," Moon replied. "The only way to control them is by cunning. Meet me here when I am again in this very same spot. I shall think of something by then."

Every day, the people withstood the heat of the nine suns as best they could. Chewing on betel leaves helped prevent the dryness in their mouths. On the twenty-seventh night, the people again gathered on the plain to wait for the full moon. Moon came as promised, and she had a plan in mind. "I cannot tell you what I plan, but, tonight, please bring me as many betel leaves as you can."

Each person went home to bring his or her own supply of betel. "Thank you," Moon said. "Now go home, because I have much work to do."

First, she gathered all her mist banks and hid her ten thousand stars behind them. Then, she began to chew the betel leaves. As the red juice dripped from her mouth and chin, she

spit it all over the sky. She kept chewing and spitting until it was time to go home. Just about then, Father Sun appeared followed closely by his eight sons.

The sight that greeted Father Sun was blood-red all over. Red dripped from Moon's chin, covered the horizon, and colored the sky. "Who was slaughtered?" he asked. "And how many?"

Moon grinned while drooling red juice down her chin. "I ate all my children," she said.

"You ate your stars?" Father Sun asked. "How did they taste?" His face showed disbelief mixed with a savage hunger.

"Simply wonderful!" Moon replied. "Why don't you eat your children, too?"

No sooner had Moon suggested this than Father Sun opened his mouth and swallowed his eight sons, one after the other.

With the strength of eight sons to add to his own, Father Sun became stronger and burned more intensely, but he was alone. He soon found out that Moon had tricked him, that she did not eat the stars.

Father Sun was angry at Moon for tricking him, and he regretted eating his eight sons. He chased Moon across the skies to punish her. When he finally caught her, he diminished her size. Moon escaped and scurried to hide from Father Sun, but eventually she reappeared to grow again.

The people of Batak say that the moon tries to keep a step ahead of Father Sun, but he always catches her. Although he reduces her in size and power, she hides and escapes to grow again.

NOTES

This story from the people of Batak on the island of Sumatra explains why there is only one sun and why the sun chases the moon.

The Batak are people who live in the Lake Toba region in north-central Sumatra. They believed that Mulojadi, or Mula Jadi Na Bolon, was the creator and Lord of the Universe.

The chewing of betel is a common practice among various Southeast Asian peoples. It is used as a gesture of welcome among friends. The betel leaf is mildly stimulating, and chewing it produces a plentiful supply of brick-red saliva, which the moon, in this story, used to create the illusion of a bloody slaughter.

The Buffalo Wins!

HUNDREDS of years ago, many of the islands around Java were ruled by a powerful king. He was not satisfied with his vast possessions; he wanted to add the entire island of Sumatra to his kingdom. He sent a message to the people of West Sumatra.

"I am now ruler of all these islands around you. Your island will soon be added to my kingdom. Surrender now or I will come with my men to conquer you."

The people of West Sumatra were alarmed. "The king of Java has thousands of men," they said. "We are no match for him. If we go to war, we are sure to lose. All our men will be killed and the women made slaves. We must think of a way to avoid war."

Everyone agreed, but no one came forth with a solution that was acceptable to all. After much discussion, a villager suggested that the battle be between buffaloes, with each side bringing a buffalo to the field. The buffaloes would battle each other and the outcome of that fight would determine winner and loser. If the buffalo belonging to the king of Java won, then the people of Sumatra would surrender to the king and become his subjects. If the buffalo belonging to the people of Sumatra won, then the Javanese king would leave them alone to continue to be free.

The king's messenger took this proposal back to his king. The king and his men agreed. "We have strong buffaloes and many splendid specimens to choose from," they said, very confident of the outcome.

So it was set.

The king sent his men all over his kingdom to look for the biggest, meanest, most powerful buffalo. When they found it, they brought it to Sumatra to groom for the coming battle.

The people of Sumatra heard about the buffalo and again gathered to discuss their strategy. They were worried. After rejecting many suggestions, they were even more disheartened. Then a farmer said, "I have a buffalo calf that is still with its mother. Why can't we take it from its mother and..." Everyone cheered!

The calf was taken from its mother. Sharpened pieces of metal were attached to its horny sheaths to make them look like horns. On the third day, a messenger ran to the Javanese camp to let the king know that they were now ready for battle.

The Javanese brought their huge, magnificent buffalo to the battlefield. It looked mean, powerful, and impatient. The Sumatrans brought a scrawny, bleating calf that could hardly stand steady on its four legs. The king's men looked at the calf and laughed out loud.

The big buffalo and the calf eyed each other across the field. The buffalo saw a wobbly-legged calf and did nothing. The calf's vision settled on a buffalo shape, which appeared to resemble its mother. It ran across the field and nudged the belly of the buffalo, looking for milk. The metal-tipped "horns," sharpened to knife points, pierced the belly of the huge buffalo. No matter where the buffalo ran, the calf followed it. The mighty buffalo bled profusely and fell down and died.

"We have been tricked!" the king of Java said, his hands clenched in fists, while the people of Sumatra rose and cheered, *"Minangkabau! Minangkabau!* The buffalo wins! The buffalo is victorious!"

The king of Java kept his promise and left Sumatra. The people remained free and called their land "The Buffalo's Victory" or "Minangkabau."

NOTES

This popular legend is told and retold even to this day. The story is set at a time in Indonesian history when the great Javanese kingdoms wanted to take over the rural villages of Sumatra in order to extend their own territorial boundaries.

Minangkabau today is a district in West Sumatra. The village is characterized by houses with roof lines that sweep up at both ends, just as the horns of the buffalo do. The women wear a headdress that appears to symbolize the horns of buffalo.

The word *"minangkabau"* comes from *"minang,"* victory, and *"kerbau,"* buffalo, meaning "the buffalo wins" or "the buffalo is victorious."

The Crocodile and the Monkey

BUAYA the crocodile lived a pleasant life. The river was large, its sandy banks were comfortable for basking in the sun, and a palm tree with his favorite coconuts grew on those banks. Every day he had a short distance to swim in order to do everything he liked doing.

One day Buaya's peace was shattered with the arrival of Beruk the monkey. With noisy chatter and squeals, Beruk climbed to the top of the coconut tree and promptly picked every ripe coconut and ate all of them. Observing this from below, Buaya became angry. "All my coconuts!" he muttered. "That monkey is eating them. There won't be any food left for me. I must stop him. But how?"

Buaya could not climb and Beruk did not swim, so one did not go near the tree and the other did not approach the water. The crocodile decided that the only way to stop the monkey was to trick him. Buaya thought about this problem for several days before an idea dawned on him.

When Beruk came to the tree one morning, Buaya called to him in a friendly voice. "Hello, dear friend!" he said. "How are you today?"

Beruk was startled to hear a crocodile speak in such a friendly voice to him.

"Since you started to come here," the crocodile said, "I have noticed that you have a happy life. How lucky you are!"

"Yes," the monkey answered. "My life is pleasant, and I like it here."

"Oh, how I envy you," the crocodile moaned. "I have so many troubles. I wish my life could be as happy as yours."

"What troubles do you have?" Beruk asked, immediately sympathetic.

"So many," Buaya replied, "that I wouldn't know where to begin. But right now there is one big problem."

"What is that?" Beruk asked.

"Can you help me if I tell you?" Buaya asked.

"Of course," the monkey said. "Just tell me."

The crocodile shed a few tears before he went on. "My father is very ill."

"Ah," the monkey answered in a truly compassionate voice. "Is he taking medicine for his illness?"

"Yes," Buaya answered. "I am going to take some to him right now. Would you like to come with me?"

"Of course, I'll come," Beruk said. "Where does he live?"

"On the other side of the river, a little ways down."

"Then I can't go. I don't swim," Beruk said.

"That's no problem," Buaya said. "If you will climb on my back and hold on, I'll take you across."

Without a moment's hesitation Beruk jumped on Buaya's back and off they went across the river. When they were about halfway across, the crocodile slowed his speed and said, without a trace of friendliness in his voice, "Beruk, my father is seriously ill and can be cured only by medicine made from the heart and intestines of a monkey. So, although it hurts me a great deal, I must kill you to save my father."

Beruk realized that he had been tricked. This is it, he thought. If I don't think of a way out, he'll swallow me in the next minute.

"If your father is so ill and must have my heart and intestines to be cured, then I shall gladly give them to you," the monkey said. "But I don't have them with me. I left my heart and intestines hanging on the top of the coconut tree. They are safer there than in my body, you see. But if you don't mind swimming back, I'll fetch them for you."

The crocodile, large in body but small in brain, turned around without a second thought and headed back to the shore. The monkey jumped off the crocodile's back and onto the coconut tree. He climbed to the top of the tree and shouted down to the crocodile, "Buaya, how stupid you are! You had food in your mouth and you spit it out."

The crocodile realized that he had been tricked by the monkey. Ashamed and angry, he disappeared into the muddy waters of the river.

NOTES

The monkey in Eastern literature is generally depicted as being clever and shrewd.

Hindu myths, which came to Sumatra many years before Islam, left their imprint on the people's beliefs long after Hinduism was gone.

Hindu mythology reveres the monkey by giving it a special place. For example, in the mythic tale of Lutung Kasarung, the black, long-haired monkey is the disguise taken by Guru Minda, son of gods. In *The Ramayana*, Hanuman, the white monkey god, leads a monkey army and performs feats of unbelievable daring to find and rescue Sinta.

In Javanese mythology, Hanuman is said to be the son of the God of Wind.

An Honest Man

WHO but an honest man would give up the chance to have the wealth and power of a king? Aman Jempret was honest to a fault. He also had abundant faith in other people's honesty.

Aman Jempret lived with his wife Inen in a small hut. With a basket in one hand and a sack under her arm, Inen Jempret was a familiar sight to the early risers in their village. Just before dawn every day, she walked through the village to the rice shed to gather the bits and pieces of rice left from the threshing of the day before. Inen and Aman Jempret did not own any fields of their own, and they did not have enough money to buy rice. What Inen could gather every morning was all the rice they had. She then walked back to their house, which was badly in need of repair.

By the time Inen reached home, her husband Aman Jempret would be gone to the river with a fish trap slung over his shoulder. Fish from the river and edible fern leaves picked on his way home completed the meals of Aman and Inen Jempret.

Without children, there was a great emptiness in their lives, but, uncomplaining, both accepted the poverty and loneliness as God's will. Sometimes their situation worried Inen Jempret, and at these times she spoke sharply to Aman and became impatient with him.

One evening after dinner, Aman Jempret said, "Inen Jempret, I have a different plan for tomorrow—different from what I've been doing every day."

Inen Jempret came from behind the wall that separated the

kitchen from the rest of the house. She was not in the mood to listen to plans and so she said, as she sat facing him, "So?" She looked at the sleeves that were pushed up over her elbows and began to unroll them carefully, smoothing out the wrinkles. She showed no interest in what Aman had to say. He repeated, "Inen Jempret, I have some special plans for tomorrow."

"You have already said that!" she replied with a frown on her face and sharpness in her tone.

"As I walked home today, I thought of a plan," he said.

"If you think too much," Inen Jempret said, "you'll forget to do what you're supposed to do."

"Never fear," Aman Jempret replied. "I set the fish trap where large trees grow."

"And what has that to do with me?" Inen Jempret snapped.

"Tomorrow I shall tie the fish trap to the top of the tallest tree."

"What! Are you out of your mind?" Inen Jempret exclaimed. "You are going fishing at the tops of trees? What fish swims in the air?" Inen Jempret asked. "You are mad."

"Perhaps," Aman Jempret answered, "but I expect to catch something."

Inen Jempret said nothing. She was so annoyed at her husband's absurd plan.

Aman Jempret, knowing he had upset his wife, decided to say nothing more of his plans. But he was up earlier than usual the next day. Before leaving the house, he made a cone from shreds of bamboo pieces. He took this with him.

Inen Jempret watched him go and thought of the embarrassment they would face when other villagers found out that Aman Jempret went fishing in treetops.

That day, she went about her regular chores. After she had picked over the milled rice, she gathered fern leaves, because she was not sure what to expect from Aman Jempret today. The leaves were washed and ready, the rice was cooked, and Inen Jempret sat in the kitchen, waiting for her husband's return.

Suddenly, she heard the sound of running feet. She leaned over to look out her door, wondering who it might be. It was Aman Jempret with excited anticipation in his eyes. Panting, he asked his wife, "Is he here yet? He said he'd be here before me!"

"Who?" Inen Jempret asked with a sinking feeling in her heart. She did not understand Aman's behavior. "Who is coming?"

"The hornbill!" Aman replied. "He said he would come." His eyes were now glued to the sky above them.

"What hornbill? Why should a hornbill come to our house?" Inen Jempret asked, thinking that her husband had really lost his sanity.

Aman Jempret now frowned and cried out, "A cheat! That's what the hornbill is!"

Inen Jempret was worried about her husband. "What has happened to you? Since yesterday you are acting and talking so strangely."

"I'm not mad," Aman Jempret said. "While we were both on top of the tree, the hornbill promised me so." He glanced at his wife and caught her disbelieving look.

"I can tell you don't believe me," he said. "Let me tell you the whole story. I caught a hornbill in the bamboo snare I made this morning. Soon after I tied the snare to the treetops, I hid in the bushes underneath. In a very short time I heard the sound of flapping wings. A hornbill was caught in the snare. I climbed up the tree and held on to the hornbill. It said, 'It's not necessary to hold me. I promise to come to your house to meet you.' I believed him."

"You really believed him?" Inen exclaimed. "You are stupid. What bird would sacrifice its life to you or any other hunter?"

"Maybe I am stupid. But I believe others speak the truth," Aman Jempret answered.

The next morning he set out with his snare again. He was determined to catch that bird and show it no mercy. The fact that his wife had called him stupid made him angry at the hornbill. Hour after hour, he waited in the bushes under the trees, but the hornbill did not come. Aman Jempret eventually fell asleep.

Vaguely, he heard the flapping of wings. He became fully awake and rubbed his eyes. There was the hornbill, trapped in his snare again! He quickly climbed the tree and grabbed it around its neck.

"Now that I have you, you dishonest liar, don't expect me to let you go!"

"Please," the hornbill said in a strangled voice. "Forgive me."

Aman Jempret tightened his hold on the hornbill's neck. "I let you go once," he said, "but not a second time. Not when you don't keep your promise!"

With a great effort, the hornbill said, "I shall give you whatever you want, if—"

"If what?" Aman Jempret said, loosening his grip slightly.

"If you can forgive me, sir. Anything that I can possibly give you, I will."

"Liar! You expect me to believe you? You can't deceive me a second time."

"I promise not to go back on my word," the hornbill said. Aman Jempret further loosened his grip around the hornbill's throat. "Please come and visit my house when you can," the hornbill continued. "Go west, cross seven rivers, turn neither left nor right, and you will reach my house."

As the hornbill spoke, Aman Jempret listened intently and gradually loosened his grip on its throat. The hornbill waited for the right moment before taking to the skies. It flew west over the horizon, and Aman Jempret watched it go.

He climbed down to the ground and started homeward. With his head hanging in dejection, he walked home, feeling the complete fool for allowing a bird to deceive him twice.

When he reached home, his wife was waiting for him at the door. "Aman Jempret!" she said in a loud voice. "Where did you steal all this?"

Aman was bewildered. He couldn't believe what he heard. "What are you saying?" he asked.

"Don't pretend you know nothing about this!" she said.

Aman Jempret became angry. "Who's pretending ignorance? And what would I pretend for?"

Inen Jempret's voice rose as she accused him of lying. "Tell me how all of this happened to come about. We've been poor for so long, I have no desire to be wealthy at someone else's expense."

"We are not wealthy," Aman Jempret shouted, equally angry now. "I never said we were. I cannot even get respect from my household, from you. I don't have anything, not even a child of my own."

Inen Jempret watched her husband's face, and she knew he

spoke the truth. How could she doubt her husband, who had always been honest and truthful? Her face softened, as she extended her hand to him.

"Come. I want you to see this."

She led him into the house. He was amazed! The house was completely different, with furniture, carpets, and all the details of a luxurious home. Aman Jempret, when his eyes had taken in all the comforts in his home, turned to his wife and asked, "Where did this come from?"

"Forgive me. I thought you had stolen all this."

"Steal? Never!" he said. Then he thought back to the events of that day. "This afternoon, the hornbill was trapped in my snare again. He offered me anything I wanted if I would forgive him for yesterday. Since I could not think of anything right away, he promised to give me something. I think he is responsible for all this."

"I should know better than to accuse you of stealing," Inen Jempret said. "Never have I known a more honest man. Forgive me, my dear husband."

"You did not understand," he said. "But what is all that food I see there? It looks and smells delicious."

"Let's have our meal now," she said.

They sat down and had the most satisfying meal each could remember. The rice was white, each grain whole and unbroken. It was soft and moist, the way they liked it. Every dish was tasty.

The next day brought more surprises for Aman and Inen Jempret. They had fresh new clothes to wear. They could now throw away their old worn clothing.

Aman Jempret dressed carefully and decided to visit his friend the hornbill. He said good-bye to his wife and set out for the western horizon. He took seven days to cross seven rivers. He reached a beautiful village that was completely deserted. The weary traveler felt such a great loneliness here that it made him think of the village of ghosts and even of death.

He arrived at a gate, and just as he was about to step through the gateway, he saw something move in the corner. It was a tiger. It stalked Aman and bared its fangs. Although Aman trembled with fear, he did not give an inch. They had a terrible battle, but Aman found that the tiger's body felt as light as a sack of cotton, and he was able to swing the tiger around. Soon the tiger gave ground to Aman and retreated into his corner.

Full of confidence now, Aman Jempret walked through the beautiful gate only to face a buffalo running to attack him.

Fighting the buffalo as fiercely as he had fought the tiger, Aman easily turned the buffalo back so that it, too, retreated to its corner.

Aman Jempret crossed several more doorways, all guarded by terribly powerful beings. He came through with not a scratch on himself.

He finally reached a heavy locked door that opened by itself when he walked up to it. Inside, Aman Jempret saw the most exquisite hall and a man and a woman at its far end. They both got up and walked toward Aman.

"I would like to see your ruler, please," Aman said. "He invited me here."

"I believe you are looking for us," the man said.

Aman looked from one to the other in amazement, because neither the man nor the woman looked like the hornbill.

"You need not worry at all, sir," the man said, smiling warmly at him. "You are well taken care of here."

Aman listened intently, for he heard something familiar. "Your voice," he exclaimed. "I recognize it! It's the hornbill's."

The man smiled broadly at Aman and said, "Yes."

"I came especially to thank you for all our gifts. My wife and I are deeply grateful," Aman Jempret said.

The man persuaded Aman to stay and rest for seven days. Where once the village was so empty and lonely it had brought thoughts of death to Aman, it was now full of people. Everyone honored him.

When the day to depart finally arrived, Aman's friend offered him a horse to ride. Aman chose one that was lame. Given another chance to choose again, Aman refused every other horse. He rode the lame horse, and he was home in the blink of an eye.

After the horse appeared at the home of Aman Jempret, people no longer saw Inen Jempret picking over broken pieces of rice or Aman Jempret going fishing in the river. The people in the village imagined stories of the strange powers of the horse, and they envied the couple.

Even the king heard these stories and greatly desired this strange horse. He called a group of his soldiers and sent them out one night to bring this horse back to him.

The soldiers crept up to Aman Jempret's house while everyone slept. They were still a distance from the stable when the horse began to neigh loudly. This noise caused the fence posts around the stable to rise and attack the soldiers. The attack threw the soldiers into confusion. When the air cleared, the soldiers all had lumps and bumps on their heads. They reported back to the king, who blamed Aman Jempret and directed his anger at him.

This incident made the king want the horse even more. He called in two of his best commanders and a group of his strongest soldiers. He sent them to steal the lame horse.

They went to the stable one night, approaching very quietly on tip-toe. When one of the soldiers pushed the door open, a loose plank fell down. Immediately, the horse started neighing, which, in turn, woke up the fence posts. After a heated battle between the troops and the fence posts, only one commander and one soldier were left alive.

Aman Jempret had watched the fight from the beginning. So had Inen Jempret. They watched one of the men untie the lame horse and lead it away while the other survivor walked behind him.

"They fought very hard for the horse," Aman Jempret whispered to Inen, who nodded her head. They watched silently as the horse was led away.

But Aman Jempret loved his horse dearly, and he felt his heart would break. He ran out and called him by his pet name. "Cempang! Cempang!"

As soon as it heard its name, the horse pulled on the rope, strangling the soldier who held it. At the same time, it kicked the man walking behind.

By morning, the story had gone around the village that Aman Jempret had killed the king's men in a most cruel way, that the corpses still lay where they had fallen. Many curious villagers gathered around his home, where they saw the king's delegate come to investigate and to take Aman Jempret to court. Most of the onlookers looked at him with hatred in their eyes.

The king presided at court. His accusation was immediate. "Murderer!" he said, his face vengeful and unforgiving.

Aman Jempret felt compelled to answer. "I am not a murderer, my lord."

"You lie!" the king replied. "How do you explain all the corpses lying around your house?"

"I am greatly upset to see that," Aman Jempret replied, "especially the bodies of our famous generals. This makes me very sad."

"A murderer never feels sorry. Don't try to get out of being punished for this crime," the king said, "because I won't let you."

Feeling obliged to explain himself truthfully, Aman said, "I am sorry, my lord, because good commanders always sacrifice themselves for the king, although they are supposed to protect the people."

"How dare you insult me," the king said. "You shall pay for this! Listen carefully. Tomorrow, your horse will compete with the best horse in the royal stables. If you win, my entire kingdom is yours." The king held his finger up to quiet the nervous whispering among the people.

"If you lose, however," he went on, "what then, eh?"

"Whatever you wish, my lord," Aman Jempret said, feeling the necessity to say something.

"Ha, ha," the king jeered. "If you lose, *you* will be given to the people, who can do what they will with you." The people cheered loudly.

Aman Jempret hung his head.

"And your horse," the king continued, "will join the royal stables. What do you say to that! Answer me!"

"Whatever you wish, my lord," Aman Jempret said.

On the day of the competition, Aman Jempret rode his lame horse onto the oval field set aside for the race. Ahead of them trotted Mungkur Uten, the swiftest horse from the royal stables. Watching from a platform were the king and queen, smiling and confident. Unsmiling and anxious at the other end of the platform was Inen Jempret.

The race consisted of two laps around the oval track, with the first to finish being the winner. As soon as the official gave the signal, Mungkur Uten leaped forward and galloped like his tail was on fire. He was halfway around the track, and Cempang had not taken a single step! The king and queen were ecstatic, while Inen Jempret clasped her hands together and wore an anxious crease on her forehead.

When Mungkur Uten was at the three-quarter mark on his first round, Aman Jempret leaned over and whispered, "Now, Cempang." Cempang then flew down the course. By the time Mungkur Uten completed his first round, Cempang was beside him. Mungkur Uten was barely halfway through the second round when Cempang completed the two rounds and won the race!

The people who had cheered at the prospect of tearing Aman Jempret apart now cheered even more at his victory. The king and queen sank back into their chairs gloomily.

Cempang, with Aman Jempret still on his back, trotted over to Inen. Aman Jempret pulled his wife onto the horse's back behind him and waited for Mungkur Uten to finish the second round.

Then he rode up to the king. Aman and Inen Jempret slid off the horse's back. "I was willing to do as you ordered, my lord," Aman Jempret said, with respect in his voice, "but, in all honesty, kind sirs," and he addressed the people, "I am not prepared to be your king."

With that, Aman Jempret and his wife Inen and his lame horse Cempang turned to go home before a silent crowd.

Thus did Aman Jempret, an honest man, refuse the power and wealth of being king.

Notes

This story is from Aceh province in North Sumatra. Aceh is the westernmost region of Indonesia and the northernmost of the island of Sumatra.

Although the Acehnese have not always been described as being friendly, they are, in reality, a warm, gracious, and hospitable people. Honesty as displayed by Aman Jempret is a virtue highly prized by the Acehnese.

In the mythology of some of the tribes of Indonesia, the hornbill is associated with death.

For the significance of the number seven, please turn to the discussion on the *kris* in More Notes on Indonesian Culture.

The Crying Stone

A long time ago, a widow lived with her young, beautiful daughter in a village near Meninjau in West Sumatra. They were very poor. They lived in a little house near the rice field where the mother worked. Every bit of food they ate was bought through the hard manual labor of the woman.

When the widow looked at her daughter, she felt compensated for her hard work by the beauty of her daughter's face. When her daughter was young, her mother often said to her, "Your pretty face is always in my eye, and it lightens my work." So she worked a little harder in order to buy a new dress or a new trinket for her daughter.

As she grew older, the young girl did not like to spend her time at home cleaning and cooking. Because of her pretty face, which brought compliments from many people, she also became conceited about her own looks. But her mother was never upset with her. Dressed in old, worn clothes so that her daughter could have new, pretty ones, the widow continued to work hard and continued to hope that her daughter would learn to respect her mother.

Both mother and daughter went to the market together one day, mother in her old threadbare clothing and daughter in a bright, attractive dress. The young girl looked at her mother and was ashamed of the way she looked in her faded clothes. So, instead of walking with her mother, she walked two steps ahead and let her mother follow her. On the way to the marketplace and on the way home, the young girl met friends who asked, "Is this your mother?"

"No," she answered, too ashamed of her mother's appearance, "she's not my mother. She's my maid."

Each time the widow heard her daughter say this, she felt her heart breaking. She was sad and hurt to be treated like this. She was also angry at the arrogance her daughter showed. She prayed to God to punish the daughter who had not learned to respect her mother. Almost at once, the young girl's legs began to turn into stone, then her body, her arms, and last her head. God had answered the widow's prayer.

Today, people passing this statue of the young girl often see drops of water oozing out of the stone. These drops, they say, are tears being shed by the girl, who is now sorry for the way she treated her mother.

Notes

Indonesians have great respect for their parents, and they are expected to show it. Breaking this code is considered a serious enough offense to be punished by gods.

The young girl in this story did not honor her mother or show her the respect that the hard-working parent deserved. Although her punishment may appear to be unusually harsh, this story points up the importance to the Indonesian of traditional respect for parents.

The Green Princess

IN the middle of a freshwater lake in North Sumatra is an island on which the village of Lukup Panalam is located. A young and beautiful princess lived in this village long ago. Both her parents had died, and her twin brother had long since left home.

Before her parents died, they had given their daughter a most curious, intricately designed gold ring that the princess always wore. The princess' ring was one of an identical pair. The other, she was told, was owned by her twin brother.

Soon after she came of age, a very handsome young man came to the village. The princess met him, and they fell in love with each other. Because they were so much in love, they decided to get married soon.

While out on the lake in a boat one day, they started to make wedding plans. The day was drawing near, and, although they had much to discuss and decisions to make, the sun was warm and pleasant on their faces, and they were lulled by the slow rhythmic movements of the boat. A sudden glint on the young man's hand caught the princess' attention.

"Why, is that a ring you have on?" the princess asked. "I have never seen you wear one before today. May I see it?"

"Of course," he said, as he slipped off the ring.

It was a beautiful gold ring with the most unusual carvings on it. The princess studied it closely and was shocked. The ring was an exact replica of the one she had on.

"Where did you get this?" she asked.

"Before my parents died, when I was still a small boy, they

gave it to me. They told me that my twin sister will have one like it. That's why I came here, to find my sister," he said.

The princess returned his ring, then took hers off and offered it to him. "Here," she said. "Take this ring, please, my brother."

And she stepped into the waters of the lake.

Before the young man could reach out for her, the water turned green. He called her name, but there was no sign of her. Only the wind answered him by picking up the waves and tossing them against the sides of the boat, rocking it.

The young man, in turn, was shocked, as he looked at her ring. The carvings on the rings were so unique, there was no question that her ring and his were a pair.

A few days later, a huge green-skinned dragon appeared in the lake. People who lived in the village swore it was the princess, who had turned into a dragon.

Once in a while, through the years, villagers have seen this dragon again. It is usually sighted when there are young couples courting on the lake or on its shores. The villagers call it the Green Princess.

NOTES

The setting for this story is the lake known as Danau Laut Tawar in Aceh province in North Sumatra. The water in the lake today contains a great deal of seaweed and algae. There are superstitions surrounding the waters of this lake, and the local people do not swim in it.

This story is told as a reminder that incest is forbidden. The princess, who unknowingly fell in love with her own brother and was about to marry him, preferred to perish in the lake rather than to disobey the laws of society.

Java

The Origin of Thunder, Lightning, Rainbow, and Rain

A long time ago when there were no people on this earth, the only living creatures were angels. And God loved them.

Then God decided to create people, and among them was Nabi Adam whom He loved best of all. God told all the angels to give Nabi Adam due respect, which they did, except for Ijajil.

Ijajil was an angel, one of God's creatures, but he did not look like the other angels, nor did he behave like any of them. He was big and heavy, his nose was round and prominent, and his eyes were shifty. Unlike the other angels, he had a mean and cruel nature. He also disobeyed God frequently.

One day, God asked the angels to leave a seat vacant for Adam. Everyone moved to leave the seat next to God, because they knew how God loved Nabi Adam. Everyone, that is, except Ijajil. He sat in the empty seat next to God and refused to move. He looked at God and challenged Him without saying a word. Other angels fluttered around him in consternation.

"Ijajil," they said, "God wants that seat reserved for Nabi Adam. Didn't you hear Him? Do move, Ijajil! God will be upset."

"I don't care," Ijajil answered. He looked defiantly at God.

"Ah, Ijajil," God said, "you disobey me again. How can I teach you a lesson? I'm afraid I will have to ask you to leave us." And so Ijajil was expelled from heaven.

Ijajil was very angry and blamed Nabi Adam. He wandered

over the earth, looking for Adam. When he found him, he said, "With you, Nabi Adam, I will always lose. But be careful. Your grandchildren will fight among themselves and be destroyed."

One of the angels overheard Ijajil and followed him, saying, "Now I see your bad character, Ijajil. You disobeyed God and now you want to destroy Nabi Adam's grandchildren. You deserve to be expelled from heaven."

"What business is it of yours what I do and don't do?"

"It is the business of angels to carry out God's wishes and to see that all His creatures are cared for," the angel said. "Have you forgotten so soon?"

Their angry voices reached the ears of other angels. They gathered around Ijajil, and several urged him to challenge the angel whereas others felt that the matter was not worth fighting over. As they argued, their voices grew louder until they were heard for many miles around. The rumbling of these voices bounced back and forth among the tops of mountains and over the treetops. People in the path of these sounds covered their ears and called this noise "thunder."

Ijajil, who had the slyness of the devil, did not want to face the angel to argue with him. He also knew that his own supernatural powers were matched by those of the angel. For example, the angel possessed a tongue that could extend a long distance and also light a fire. So, while everyone argued, he slipped off to hide inside the trunk of a huge banyan tree.

The angel caught sight of Ijajil slipping into the tree. As he ran after Ijajil, his tongue lashed out, shining red and white, to strike the tree with fire. But Ijajil knew the angel's intention and ran from the tree just as the fire tongue struck it and burned it down. This fire tongue lit up the skies, and people oohed and aahed in wonder and fright and called it "lightning."

While Ijajil ran from the angel, he tried to trick the angel even as God watched them from heaven. God knew that the fight would never end because both Ijajil and the angel possessed supernatural powers. So God sent all the angels in heaven to stop the fight. By using a colorful ladder that they called a "rainbow," the angels descended to earth.

They went to the angel first and begged the angel to stop.

"Never!" the angel replied. "Ijajil has flaunted his mean nature and disobeyed God too often. He deserves to be taught a lesson. I will not stop until he promises to change. Otherwise, he must die."

The angels then went to Ijajil to beg him to stop.

"I will be killed if I stop fighting," he said.

"No, no!" the angels answered in a chorus. "Just promise you will change, and no one will harm you."

"Ha, why should I change?" Ijajil demanded. "Why should *you* not change to be like me?"

"No, no!" the angels cried out again. "We will not change. But if *you* do not, you cannot return to heaven with us. Please, Ijajil, do stop this fighting."

Ijajil turned his back on them and refused to say more. The angels hung their heads as they slowly made their way up the rainbow to heaven. They clustered around God and the angels cried. They cried so much that the tears overflowed and dropped to earth, where people called it "rain."

Now everyone despaired that this fight would ever end. Ijajil and the angel both had supernatural powers and both could not die.

But God decreed that the fight would finally end when the sun rose from the west and the moon from the north and the earth stopped spinning. The day the fight ends, God said, will be called "doomsday."

And so the fight between the two supernatural beings goes on even to this day. We know this, because we still have thunder, lightning, rainbow, and rain.

NOTES

This legend provides a different explanation of four elements of weather. A discussion of the climate of Indonesia may be found in More Notes on Indonesian Culture.

References to "Nabi Adam" indicate Islamic influence in this story. In the Koran, the Islamic equivalent of the Bible, three prophets from the Christian New Testament and twenty-two, including Adam, from the Old Testament, are included. To the Muslims, who practice Islam, the last and greatest prophet is Mohammed. Mohammed is so revered that he is the only one, besides Jesus, the Muslims call "Prophet." Others are called "Nabi," a title given to a representative of God.

Kerta's Sin

LONG ago, there were men, like Pak Miam, whose job it was to gather the nests of swiftlets nestled under ledges among steep, slippery rocks facing the restless waters of the South Sea. Theirs was a dangerous profession. The ocean along the coastline was never calm. Furious storms frequently churned the water, striking fear even into the hearts of seasoned mariners. Everyone knew that Ratu Lara Kidul ruled the South Sea and woe befell the person who did not make a sufficient sacrificial offering to her before venturing out!

Like all the other gatherers, Pak Miam went to work by lowering himself on coconut fiber ropes over the wet rocks above the water in order to reach the nests. He clambered from ledge to ledge just above the grasping fingers of the waves. He was one of the strongest and bravest of pickers, and his wife and son were proud of him.

One day, his son Kerta said, "I have long fingers and strong hands, Father. Why can't I go and help you and become a picker?"

"You are almost ten now, Kerta," his father answered, "but that is still too young for this kind of work. The gathering season will begin soon, and if you wish, you may carry the sacrificial offering for me on the first day."

"It is much too dangerous," Kerta's mother said. "He is too young to go near the rocks."

"He will not go to the rocks," Pak Miam said. "He will carry the offering to the palm forest where the priests will be waiting. There, our offering of food will be placed on a white mat and the priests will pray for us."

"I shall cook a large and most delicious meal to offer the goddess of the South Sea," Kerta's mother said. "She will certainly bless you and keep you safe while you work throughout the season."

When the first day of the season arrived, Kerta proudly accompanied his father to work, bearing a cloth-covered bundle holding his father's sacrificial offering of rice and chicken that his mother had prepared.

On this first day of gathering birds' nests, the pickers went to the rocks earlier than usual so they could offer their food to Ratu Lara Kidul. The men fasted until after the offering, eating only after she had eaten.

Pak Miam was accustomed to this fasting, but Kerta was not. He complained.

"Father," he said, "I am so hungry! Why can't I eat some of the food I am carrying? I can smell the chicken. It smells so good!"

"We must not eat the queen's food," Pak Miam explained. "The queen of the South Sea will become very angry and cause terrible things to happen to us."

"What sort of things?" Kerta asked, curious.

"I don't know," his father answered, "because it has never happened to me. But the queen is quick to anger. She must have her sacrifice. If you can wait a little longer, as soon as you have placed our offering on the white mat, I will buy you whatever you want to eat from the *warung* people who cook with little stoves along the path."

Kerta trudged silently behind his father. The aroma rising from the bundle in his hands tempted him so much he could not keep his mind off food. He became hungrier and hungrier until his little fingers could no longer resist exploring within the cloth covers. He felt a piece of chicken in his fingers and wriggled it out without letting his father know. Kerta ate the chicken; it tasted delicious! But the chicken, far from satisfying his hunger, only succeeded in whetting his appetite. His fingers quickly found their way back under the cloth and discovered some rice.

Soon Kerta and Pak Miam arrived at the palm forest where the priests waited for the sacrificial offerings.

"Unwrap the food and give it to the priest. He will place it on the white mat," Pak Miam said. "Then come and choose whatever you want from the *warung*."

The priest took his offering and placed it on the white mat alongside other offerings. Kerta saw how small and meager his meal looked. Next to some large, generous offerings, his looked even smaller. He stole a look at the priest's face, but it showed neither pleasure nor disapproval. The priest made no comment. Kerta sighed with relief; he was glad that this duty was done.

When his father bought food for him to eat, Kerta found that he was not very hungry. He watched Pak Miam and the others prepare for work, securing their bags and tightening their cords. One by one, each man lowered himself on ropes that swayed in the wind over the sheer rocks. When at last Pak Miam had dropped from view, Kerta wandered through the palm forest. With a full stomach, he soon became very drowsy. Picking a spot between two trees, he lay down in a place where his father was sure to see him when he returned.

He felt he had just dropped off to sleep when he heard a voice. "Are you ready to go home, Father?" he asked, rubbing his eyes.

"I am not your father," the man answered. "The sun is almost gone. Your father must have returned with the men. Best run home, boy. The waves are thrashing the rocks. A bad storm is coming. Ratu Lara Kidul must be very angry tonight."

Kerta ran home to the village, where the storm had already started to rattle the walls and roofs of the houses.

"Where is your father?" his mother asked.

"Is he not home yet?" Kerta asked. "I fell asleep, and the man who woke me up said that he must have left with all the other men. There was no one left."

"Then do not worry," his mother said. "He is safe and will come home soon."

That night, Kerta dreamed of an ugly woman with long hair streaming and writhing like eels around her face, with huge, bloodshot eyes and a big, bulbous nose. She fixed him with a glare and accused him of eating her food.

"Because of you," she said, "your father is in the Cave of Squids. He will die there!" As she reached out to grab him with her slimy, slippery arms, Kerta screamed. He woke up and found his mother awake, still waiting for his father. He told her of his dream.

"Did you eat the food offering?" his mother asked with horror and fear in her voice.

"Some of it, Mother," Kerta answered.

His mother wept and wailed.

Finally, she said, "We have much to do tomorrow, Kerta, if we are to save your father. Go to sleep. There is nothing we can do now."

Kerta fell into a troubled sleep. This time he dreamed of a beautiful lady who did not threaten him but spoke gently with kindness in her voice.

"You must go and free your father," she said. "I will forgive you if you do as I say. First, go to the Cave of Masjid Sela, the Mosque of Connection. My servant will be there to help you reach the Cave of Squids."

Kerta woke up and again told his mother of his dream. "I must go and bring Father home," he said. His mother did not try to stop him. In the growing light of day, Kerta sought other pickers, his father's co-workers, and wise old fishermen.

"Where is the Cave of Squids?" he asked them. "How do I get there? Where is the Cave of Masjid Sela?"

When he had learned all that the elders could tell him, Kerta walked to the edge of the village to look for the steep rock face, where he would find the opening to the first cave. Here, the rocks rose from the waters of an inland sea. The wind continued to whip the waves into fierce foam below, paralyzing young Kerta.

He tore his eyes from the ocean and concentrated on gaining entrance to the Cave of the Mosque of Connection. Step by step, he lowered himself on a rope to the cave opening, holding on to the same slippery ledges that Pak Miam had held. The wind buffeted him against the rocks and tried to shake him loose from his rope. Kerta held on and inched his way to the cave.

Upon entering the dimly lit cave, he saw, close to the entrance, a mound of rocks marking a tomb. Beyond the tomb, he made out a narrow opening leading into the grotto. If that is the passage to the Cave of Squids, he thought, I can never squeeze myself through it. Dismay overwhelmed him.

Then he saw a bright light far back in the cave. It came from a strange old man with a white beard and hands as transparent as glass, who looked as cold as crystal. He walked carefully and slowly toward Kerta. In a voice that sounded like the tinkle of a dozen tiny bells, he asked, "How can I help you, my son?"

Kerta told him of the sin he had committed. "Because of me, my father is now in the Cave of Squids and I must rescue him."

"Your sin is great, my son. Several hundred years ago, I also displeased Ratu Lara Kidul," the Glass Man said in his tinkling voice, "so I am doomed to stay here. Once in a hundred years, she permits me to take this form to help someone. Tonight is such a time. But I have only until dawn. When the first light of day reaches over the horizon, I must return to my tomb for another hundred years. I will help you. To call me, you need only shout, 'Help me, holy man.'"

He passed his icy hands of glass over the boy's eyes. Kerta felt his body grow long and felt himself close to the ground. He looked at his hands and his body and found scales on himself and four short legs. He had been changed to a monitor lizard.

"Remember," the Glass Man said, "I have only until dawn. I cannot help you after that."

As a lizard, Kerta was able to slide through the narrow passage from the Cave of the Mosque of Connection to the Cave of Squids.

He looked at the large cave filled with octopuses and squids of all sizes and varieties. He knew that he had only hours to find his father and return to the first cave by dawn.

He scurried to the ceiling of the Cave of Squids to get a better view behind the creatures and in the crevices. He slipped to the floor of the grotto and slithered among the creatures, looking for his father's familiar figure. All the while, the roar of the waves at the cave entrance worsened.

At last, after what seemed like several hours, Kerta sighted his father in a dark corner of the cave. He hurried to him, and when he touched his father, he, also, turned into a monitor lizard. But Pak Miam was exhausted from his many attempts to escape from the cave and the long tentacles of the giant octopus. He was barely conscious and did not respond. Kerta tried to awaken him, but it was hopeless. He half-dragged and half-carried his father out of the corner toward the passage. Because of his father's weight, Kerta had to stop and rest more and more often.

Progress was slow, but as they inched their way to the passage, giant octopuses rose up as if on command. With long, flailing arms, they moved toward the pair. In one way or another, Ratu Lara Kidul appeared to be determined to have her sacrificial offering.

"Help me, holy man!" Kerta yelled.

The giant octopuses all sank to the bottom of the grotto. Outside, the wind howled more fiercely as Ratu Lara Kidul gave vent to her anger and frustration.

When he finally reached the passage, Kerta was near collapse. With his last ounce of strength, he called to the Glass Man once more. The Glass Man appeared promptly and brought Pak Miam through the passage and turned him back into his human form.

Kerta, meanwhile, had made his way into the passage before slipping into unconsciousness. The Glass Man called to him, "My son! Where are you? You must hurry because my time is almost up!" Pak Miam reached in to pull him through the passage. "Kerta, hold on to my finger and I shall pull you through."

Kerta did not hear them. When dawn sent its first tentacles of light into the cave, the Glass Man returned to his tomb for another hundred years.

Pak Miam buried his face in his hands and sank to the floor of the cave. He sorrowed over Kerta and remained in this position for a long time.

"Do not grieve, Father," Kerta said, coming slowly out of the passage. "This was all my fault. If I had been saved today, Ratu Lara Kidul would still have demanded a sacrifice. I do not mind being the sacrifice to her." The lizard slipped out of the cave onto the slippery rocks.

Kerta was doomed to live the rest of his days as a lizard.

NOTES

The monitor lizard, the form Kerta was made to assume in his search for his father, is a type of lizard that is a close relative of the snake. It has a long neck and the darting tongue of the snake. Indonesia has two types of monitor lizards: the *biawak* and the komodo dragon.

There is an open area of no land between the islands of Indonesia and the South Pole. The south shore of these islands consists of long stretches of inaccessible rock indented by an inland sea.

The edible nests of swiftlets are highly desired by the Chinese, but a bird's-nest gatherer works in constant danger. From the top of the rocks, gatherers like Pak Miam lowered themselves to a bamboo platform that was built above a cave in which birds roosted. They then waited on the platform for the right wave to come. They dropped into it and swept into the cave on the wave. After gathering the nests, usually in the dark, they depended again on another wave to carry them out and up on a swell. They had to catch the rope in the split second that they were lifted, if they wanted to return safely.

In Central Java, many beliefs about a mythical queen persist to this day. She lives in the Palace of Ghosts in the Indian Ocean in the South Sea off the island of Java. This queen is believed to be beautiful and is known as Roro Kidul or Lara Kidul. A Javanese goddess, she demanded offerings and punished those who did not give her her full measure, just as she punished Kerta for eating her food.

For additional information on Roro Kidul, see More Notes on Indonesian Culture.

Tiung Wanara

SEVERAL hundred years ago, Chepaka, a wise man who lived in the mountains of Pajajaran, was rumored to know the answer to everything. People in the villages made the long trek to his mountain home to seek his advice. The king of Pajajaran at that time was Prabu Mundang Wangi. He was a cruel ruler, and his people feared him. The king decided to test this sage to see whether he really did know all the answers. He sent for Chepaka.

He instructed the queen to hold a copper basin in front of her stomach under her sarong in order to give the appearance of being with child. When the sage came, he was to be asked what she was carrying, a boy or a girl.

Before they could ask Chepaka, he already knew their question. "Your Majesty will have a son," he said.

Immediately the king called his guards. "Guards! Kill this imposter!" he said. "The queen is not with child."

His men did not want to harm a wise man and would not move to touch Chepaka. The king shouted at them, but to no avail. Red in the face and bursting with ill temper, the king turned to Chepaka and banished him from his kingdom. "Leave at once and never come back!" he ordered.

"I will go," Chepaka said, "but let me say that I never said the queen is pregnant *now*. She will bear a son in the near future whose name will be Siung Wanara. He will grow up to kill you."

The king scoffed at his prophecy, but the more he thought about it, the more he brooded over it. Soon after, the queen did become expectant and did give birth to a boy.

By this time, the king had decided what must be done. He summoned a maidservant caring for the queen. "Bring the baby to me when the queen is sleeping. Tell no one what you are doing."

The maidservant was frightened of the king and so obeyed him without question and told no one.

Then the king placed the baby in a basket and called one of his men to his side. "Take this infant to the mouth of the river. Kill him and throw him in," he instructed.

The servant did not dare refuse. He took the baby and carried the bundle of life to the side of the River Krawang. He gazed at the river in its turbulent rush to join the sea.

He looked at the baby, then at the eddies in the river, and he could not throw him into the water. He fell to his knees and prayed to the Sea God Kyai Belorong.

"What shall I do with the prince? I cannot throw him in the water as the king has ordered me to do," he said. "I cannot destroy such an innocent thing. Tell me what to do. Give me some sign." He prayed with the newborn prince held close to his chest.

Soon the current rushing before him and the boom of the surf in the distance came together in a voice that spoke to him.

"Put the child in a cave along the shore," the voice said. "Tell your king that you have placed the prince in the hands of Kyai Belorong."

The man searched for a dry cave above the high-water mark. There he left the prince in his basket and returned to his king.

"Your Majesty," he said, "the little prince is now in the hands of the god Kyai Belorong."

"Well done!" the king said, rubbing his hands together in satisfaction.

There was great sadness in the palace because of the disappearance of the infant prince. The queen went into a steady decline and soon died.

Meanwhile, Kyai Belorong called to the poor fisherman Kaiman. Many times he had heard Kaiman pray to Brahma for a child of his own. Kaiman and his wife Rasula were poor, but they wanted a baby of their own so badly that they prayed for a child day and night, every day.

While Kaiman slept that night, a voice instructed him, "Go

to the River Krawang and follow its shore till you come to the caves near the ocean. Go to the first cave above the high-water mark."

Kaiman was astonished, but he was positive that the voice had clearly said all of this to him. Without saying anything to Rasula, he set off to look for the cave in the morning. As he neared it, he heard the baby's cries of hunger. When he reached the cave, he found a baby boy dressed in silk and wrapped in a rich blanket. Amazed, he lifted the basket and took it home to Rasula.

When she saw Kaiman coming home with a bundle in his arms, Rasula said, "What are you carrying that is so precious? Surely, it cannot be gold!"

"More precious than gold," he answered. "See what Brahma has given us. Our prayers are answered!"

Rasula lifted the blanket and could hardly believe her eyes. "Brahma heard our prayers," she whispered.

In a few months, Prabu Mundang Wangi married again and worried no more about a son named Siung Wanara. His second queen gave him two more sons, both of whom grew up learning the cruel ways of their father. The older was named Prince Tanduran.

In spite of being very poor, Kaiman and Rasula surrounded their son with love. He grew into a good-natured lad who was handsome and carried himself with a princely bearing.

Kaiman and Rasula often marveled at their son. "Who is he? Where does he come from?" they asked each other.

"Do you think he is a prince kidnaped by his father's enemies?" Kaiman asked.

"Will he remain with us always?" Rasula wondered.

One day, as the boy and his father walked through the forest, he picked up an object lying on the side of the trail. "What is this, Father?" the boy asked.

"That is a monkey's tooth," Kaiman answered.

"I shall keep this," the boy said, turning the tooth over in his hand. "And I shall call myself Siung Wanara (Tusk-Monkey)."

Siung Wanara knew how he was adopted by the poor fisherman and his wife. It was a story he begged to be told often. One day, he asked Kaiman, "Who are my parents? Where do I come from?"

Kaiman could not answer him, but the question had bothered him more and more as the boy had grown up. So he went to see a sage.

"See that he learns to be a smith," the sage advised. "More than this I cannot tell you at this time."

So Siung Wanara went to Kaiman's kinsman, a blacksmith in the city of Pajajaran. He was apprenticed to the smith and, in time, proved to be a quick student. In a few months he was well on his way to mastering the trade. In a few years his fame had begun to spread. People admired the craftsmanship of his work and liked him for his easygoing manner.

His fame reached the ears of the king, who, like others, wanted to go and see the skillful work of this young man. When he reached the blacksmith's workshop, one look at the apprentice's face recalled the face of his first queen. The resemblance was so striking that the king watched him for a long time before asking, "What is your name? Who are your parents?"

"I don't know who I am, Your Majesty," the young man answered. "My father, Kaiman the fisherman, found me in a cave when I was a baby. He and his wife have raised me, and they are the only family I know."

The king left for his palace and immediately sent for the servant who had been ordered to kill the infant so many years ago. The servant was now an old man. He hobbled up to the king and bowed very low.

"What did you do to my eldest son? You were supposed to kill him in the River Krawang. Did you do that?" the king asked.

The old servant shook with fear. "No, Your Majesty," he said. "I did not have the heart to kill an innocent baby, so I prayed to Kyai Belorong. His voice told me to leave the child in a cave near the shore. That is what I did."

"You will die for not obeying my orders!" the king bellowed. Turning to the guards, he said, "Execute him!"

Then he called for his soldiers. "Bring the fisherman Kaiman to me!"

Kaiman walked with escorts to the palace and bowed very low before the king and practically crawled to his feet. He was trembling so much with fear that he could not have walked upright even if he had wanted to. When he peeped at the king's face, he trembled even more. The king looked very grim and he spoke harshly to Kaiman. "Where did you find your adopted son?" he asked.

"I found him in a cave along the shore, Your Royal Majesty," Kaiman answered.

"Why did you let him learn a smith's trade? It is a prince's trade," the king said.

"My kinsman needed an assistant and offered to take him as an apprentice," Kaiman said. The king was silent for a long moment. Apparently satisfied that Kaiman spoke the truth and knew nothing of the matter, he dismissed him.

"Go home to your village," he said.

When Kaiman reached home, he described the interrogation and the king's behavior to Rasula.

"Do you think," Rasula said, "that our son is a prince of an enemy kingdom?"

"I don't know what to think," Kaiman said. "I must go and see the Wise One again. He may be able to tell us."

Early the next morning Kaiman went to see the sage. He told him of the king's summons, the questions he had asked, and the king's agitation.

"Why?" Kaiman asked. "Is our son known to the king in some way? Is he in danger from the king?"

"Refresh yourself and rest now," the sage said. "Then I shall tell you about your son."

When the sage was finally ready to speak, he said, "Before the prince was born, the king was told that his eldest son would kill him one day. Afraid of this prophecy, he ordered his servant to kill the infant son, but his servant could not make himself do it. Instead, he placed the baby in a cave, where you found him."

Kaiman listened, his worst fears confirmed. He did not know what to do.

"Wait for the right moment to tell your son the truth," the Wise One said. "He must beware of his younger brother Prince Tanduran; he has great power and much cruelty. Go to your son in Pajajaran now before going home."

When Kaiman reached the smith's shop, the king was already there. The fisherman could see that the king knew the truth.

"Is this cage strong enough to hold a tiger?" the king asked the young smith.

"Strong enough to hold ten tigers, Your Majesty," the young man answered, proud of his handiwork.

"I want you to check the whole interior of the cage before I pay you," the king insisted.

Kaiman whispered to his son. "Don't go in alone. He means to do you harm."

"You, fisherman!" the king yelled. "What are you whispering! I did not ask you to come. Go home before I have you executed."

"Your Highness," the young man said, "my father just warned me to get a good price for the cage because it is so well made. Before you pay for it, would you like to check the special bolt that I made?"

"Where is it?" the king asked.

"Inside."

The king stepped into the cage to inspect the bolt. The fisherman, who had stepped back at the king's rebuff, quickly closed the cage and slid the bolt into place.

The king shouted for his men, but Kaiman was persuasive. "Carry the cage to the river, all you good people. We will be rid of him and his tyranny. We can be free men!"

Kaiman then told of the cruel father who had sent his eldest son to be killed by a servant, how the servant could not kill an innocent babe, and how he had found the infant and raised him as his own son.

The cage with the king was thrown into the water. "Long live our new king!" the crowd shouted. The people exiled Prince Tanduran and his brother and made Siung Wanara king, naming him Tiung Wanara.

NOTES

This story is a Sundanese legend and comes from West Java.

The king's statement that the craft of a smith is a "prince's trade" refers to the position of a smith in ancient Javanese culture. The smith in those days held an honored position at court and, according to ancient Javanese chronicles, the roles of prince and smith overlapped. The smiths were supposed to have descended from the gods. The *kris* smiths, to this day, are especially honored by their fellow countrymen because their work is considered sacred, bringing them into contact with supernatural powers. More information on the *kris,* an unusual instrument of death, is included in More Notes on Indonesian Culture.

Sarong is the skirt that women wear. A further discussion may be found under Clothing in More Notes on Indonesian Culture.

Brahma is one of the most important of the Hindu gods. He is known as the creator.

"Kyai" is a form of address used with a highly respected, religious person.

Pak Dungu

NCE there lived an honest and hard-working farmer by the name of Pak Dungu. *"Dungu"* means "stupid," and everyone agreed that Pak Dungu was as slow-witted as his name suggested. His wife, who managed all the money in the family, told her husband one day that they needed more money.

"We must sell our *kerbau,* our buffalo," she said. Pak Dungu agreed; he did not disagree with her very often.

"Early tomorrow, take the *kerbau* to the market and sell it for 250 *rupiah*—not 200 but 250, do you hear?" Pak Dungu agreed again. Bu Dungu was not a wife you could easily refuse.

Unknown to them, Pak Busuk, a neighbor, overheard their conversation. He loved to play pranks on people, earning himself the name of "rascal." Now he thought of more mischief as he eavesdropped. He hurried away to look for his friends Pak Colek and Pak Cokel to ask if they would help in his mischievous plans for Pak Dungu.

Early the next morning, Bu Dungu shook her husband awake. Shivering and yawning, Pak Dungu got dressed and stepped outside into the chill air to find the *kerbau* waiting. Shaking his head to keep awake, he mumbled to himself. "Why so early? And not even a bite to eat yet. A body needs some food so early in the morning to strike a good bargain."

He had just turned the first bend in the road when he met Pak Busuk walking toward him. "Good morning, Pak Dungu," he said. "Where are you going so early?"

"To the market to sell my *kerbau,*" Pak Dungu said glumly.

"*Kerbau!*" Pak Busuk questioned. "You did say *kerbau!* But I don't see any."

"Right here!" Pak Dungu said, pointing to his buffalo. Irritably, he said, "He's so big. Are you blind?"

Pak Busuk looked at the *kerbau* from all angles and felt its body, its tail, and each leg.

"This goat a *kerbau!*" he said, bursting out in loud laughter. "Your name explains it! What do you want for this goat? I'll buy it from you for 50 *rupiah.* I can save you a trip to the market."

Pak Dungu walked off without a word. "How can he mistake a *kerbau* for a goat! Just because he thinks I'm stupid, he's trying to play a trick on me." He grumbled and mumbled to himself as he walked away.

Pretty soon he met Pak Cokel on the road.

"Good morning!" his friend said. "Where are you going with that goat?"

"This is *not* a goat! It's a *kerbau!*" Pak Dungu said indignantly.

Pak Cokel looked at him in surprise, then at the animal. "A *kerbau!* It looks like a goat to me." And he felt the animal from head to tail as he made some muffled bleating sounds like a goat.

"What are you asking for this goat?" Pak Cokel asked.

"Goat! It's a *kerbau!*" Pak Dungu said, almost shouting in reply. "Use your eyes. It's a *kerbau.* How can a goat be this size? I'm selling it for 250 *rupiah.*"

"Too much," Pak Cokel said. "The goat is too small to go for that huge sum. I don't think you can get 40 *rupiah* for this goat, but I'll buy it from you for 50 *rupiah.*"

Pak Dungu walked away, pulling his *kerbau* after him. But, his confused mind asked, was it a *kerbau!* Was it a goat? When Pak Cokel was out of sight, Pak Dungu stopped and scrutinized his animal and felt him all over. Yes, it was a *kerbau.* His wife called it a *kerbau.* It was *not* a goat. Why, then, did two men call it a goat? As he tried to muddle his way through this puzzle, he walked on, not quite sure what animal followed him.

"Good morning!" a voice hailed him. "Where are you going so early?"

Surprised, Pak Dungu looked up to see that it was Pak Colek. "To the market," he replied.

"What do you want for your goat?" Pak Colek asked.

What! thought Pak Dungu, now *he* also thinks it's a goat. Is it a *kerbau,* or is it a goat? "Two hundred fifty *rupiah,*" he answered out loud.

"Too high!" Pak Colek replied. "I'll pay you fifty for it. What do you say?"

Pak Dungu was now really confused. Bu Dungu must have been playing a joke on me when she called it a *kerbau.* It must be a goat, he thought.

"Well, Pak Dungu," Pak Colek said. "Are you going to sell me your goat? If not, I must go to the market today. I'm sure I can buy a goat for less." And Pak Colek started to move away.

Pak Dungu, still unsure of himself, said, "Pak Colek, pay me for this goat, 50 *rupiah.*"

Pak Colek counted out 50 *rupiah* and gave them to Pak Dungu in exchange for the rope tied to the animal.

When Pak Dungu reached home, Bu Dungu was cheerful and smiling, and unusually pleasant. "Back already?" she asked. "He was sold pretty fast! How lucky we are."

"Here's the money," Pak Dungu said. "I sold him before we reached the market. Yes, we were lucky."

Bu Dungu counted the money. "What! This is only 50 *rupiah,*" she said. "Where's the rest of the money?"

"That's right," Pak Dungu answered. "I could only get 50 *rupiah.* It was a goat, not a *kerbau.*"

"Fifty *rupiah* for our big *kerbau!*" she screeched. She grabbed an iron bar in her right hand and brandished it in the air. With her left hand on her hip, she stood by the door and shouted, "At your age, can't you tell the difference between a goat and a *kerbau* yet? Go back to the man who bought our *kerbau* for 50 *rupiah* and get 200 more from him. Not a *rupiah* less! Until you do, don't you dare come home!" And she shook the bar in his face.

Pak Dungu ran all the way to the market. He scolded himself for having been deceived so easily. He knew that he must get 200 more *rupiah* and, at the same time, think of a way to make the three men pay for their prank. Pak Dungu was not very bright, but the thought of facing his wife without the 200 additional *rupiah* spurred his thinking. As he approached the marketplace, he had an idea.

He went to two *warung,* or food stalls, and gave each shopkeeper a certain sum of money, saying, "I shall bring my friends here shortly. Serve them whatever they wish. Then I shall nod my head and shake this bell. When you hear it tinkle, please say, 'The bill's been paid.' Do you understand what you are to do?"

The shopkeepers, pleased to be paid in advance, readily agreed to his plan. He stopped at one more stall before he ran into Pak Busuk, Pak Cokel, and Pak Colek. They had just sold Pak Dungu's *kerbau* for 250 *rupiah* and were elated with their profit.

Pak Dungu hailed them in a most friendly way. "Come and have a snack with me in the *warung*," he said. "I'll treat, since I'm celebrating the sale of my goat."

The three men followed Pak Dungu to a *warung* and ate and drank amid a great deal of talk and laughter. When they were done, Pak Dungu asked the *warung*-keeper for his bill. "The bill is 15 *rupiah*," he said.

Pak Dungu nodded his head and shook a small bell on his cap. At the sound of the bell's tinkle, the *warung*-keeper said, "The bill's been paid, sir."

The eyes of the three men grew round with wonder. They followed Pak Dungu while keeping an eye on the *warung*-keeper, expecting him to demand payment at any moment.

Soon they came to a cigar shop where Pak Dungu bought four packets of cigars, one for each of them. He asked the shopkeeper for his bill, then nodded his head and shook his bell. The shopkeeper said, "The bill's been paid, sir."

The three men were now full of wonder. They went to another *warung* and ate and drank. When it was time to pay the bill, the same thing happened. Pak Dungu was told, "The bill's been paid, sir."

Pak Busuk could stand it no longer. "Why don't you have to pay for what you buy?" he asked.

Pak Dungu hesitated before he answered. "It is a secret," he said, then added reluctantly, "but if you promise not to tell anyone, I guess I can tell you."

All three men promised.

Lowering his voice, Pak Dungu said, "It's a magic bell my father left me. It's a wonderful thing. I never have to pay for what I buy; all I do is shake this bell. When people hear the tinkling of the bell, they think they've been paid already."

Pak Busuk could hardly hide his desire to own the bell. "I'll pay you 200 *rupiah* for it," he said.

"I could never sell it, an heirloom from my father," Pak Dungu said. "And think of the money I would lose if I didn't have it!"

"But I'll send you something every day," Pak Busuk promised. "I promise to fill your basic needs, so you really won't need the bell."

Reluctantly, Pak Dungu agreed. "I suppose, then, it's all right to sell it to you. But don't tell my wife. And pay me 250 *rupiah*."

Pak Busuk paid him the money the three swindlers had received from the sale of the *kerbau*, and Pak Dungu gave him the bell.

As soon as they were alone, the three decided to try their bell. Instead of going into one of the food stalls, a *warung*, they decided to have a meal at a restaurant. They ordered ten different courses of expensive food and ate and drank until they could hardly get up from the table.

Finally, Pak Busuk asked for the bill. "Twenty *rupiah*," the waiter said. Pak Busuk nodded his head and shook the bell. The waiter continued to stand there while Pak Busuk, Pak Cokel, and Pak Colek stood up to go. The waiter called the owner, who stopped them at the door.

"Where's your payment?" the owner asked.

Pak Busuk nodded his head and shook the bell. "You haven't paid for your meal," the owner said in a loud voice.

Pak Busuk again nodded and the bell tinkled. The owner was now becoming red in the face with anger. "Money!" he shouted. "You haven't paid!" And the more he demanded, the more Pak Busuk shook his bell.

The owner grabbed an iron bar and beat Pak Busuk and his friends until they were sore all over.

"Stupid fools!" he roared. "Who ever heard of paying for food with a bell! Get out and don't ever come back!"

NOTES

Pak Dungu, with his honest but simple mind, is clearly the underdog. He eventually outwits those who made fun of him and reaps revenge at the same time.

The fool in folklore tries very hard to act as others do. For all his effort, he usually cannot reach the level of behavior he wishes to attain. Readers often see themselves in the same situation, identify with the fool, and give him their full sympathy, thus making him one of the most, if not the most, popular of all folk characters.

"Pak" is a colloquial form of "Bapak" and means "Mr." or "Master" or "Father." "Bu" or "Ibu" can be interpreted to mean "Mother" or "Mrs."

Kerbau is the faithful, plodding buffalo that is ever present on farms in Indonesia.

Warung is a small cafe or roadside stand.

The Mosque

Iт was the year 1401. Demak Palace was the home of King Patah, but the Muslims had no "home" where they could pray and learn more about their religion. So the holy leaders of Java gathered in Demak and decided to build a large mosque to serve as the center for praying and teaching.

They petitioned King Patah, who granted them permission to build a mosque, provided they built it in one night.

So the leaders, Sunan Kali Jogo, Sunan Bonang, Sunan Ampel, Sunan Gunung Jati, Sunan Giri, Sunan Muria, Sunan Kudus, Sunan Drajat, and Sunan Syeh Siti Jenar, each took responsibility for one part of the job. Sunan Bonang, for example, was to see that most of the pillars were built. Sunan Kali Jogo was responsible for one pillar and the roof.

The night set aside for building the mosque found each man busy working on his share of the structure. Only one person, Sunan Kali Jogo, was not busy. He spent his time lolling on the floor and cooking and eating rice to satisfy his hunger.

"Why aren't you working?" Sunan Bonang asked him.

"When are you going to start?" Sunan Giri asked.

"The night is half gone, Sunan Kali Jogo. You must start working, or we will not complete the mosque in time," Sunan Gunung Jati said.

One by one, all the other holy men became upset because they were almost finished, while Sunan Kali Jogo had not yet started on his part of the mosque.

"Here it is, almost morning, and you haven't started your work yet!" they accused him.

Only then did Sunan Kali Jogo get up from the floor and begin to work.

He looked for building material for his pillar. But morning was almost upon them, and he did not have time to collect the proper material. So, instead, he gathered wood left over from the work done by the others, and putting pieces all together, tied them with some rope. The bundle made a strong pillar.

He had no time to make roof tiles. So he took all the crust left over from the rice he had cooked that night and put it on the roof in place of tiles.

"What are you doing?" the others asked him. "What kind of roof is that?"

"Patience!" he admonished them. "You'll see soon enough."

Because he was still working just before dawn, when everyone else was done, they gathered to watch him complete his work. When he finished the roof, all the other leaders were uneasy. They could see that the pillar that Sunan Kali Jogo had made was not the same height as the other pillars. While they wondered how to point out his mistake, Sunan Kali Jogo climbed to the top of the mosque. He placed his right foot on the uneven pillar at Demak Mosque (in Java) and his left foot on the pillar at the mosque in Mecca (in Saudi Arabia).

Then he stamped his right foot so that the pillar he made became the same height as the other pillars. At the same time, the pillars at Demak Mosque became the same height as those in the mosque at Mecca.

These pillars built in the fifteenth century still support the mosque at Demak on Java.

NOTES

Islam is the name of the religion founded by the Arab prophet Mohammed. A person who follows Islam is a Muslim, and Islam's place of worship (the equivalent of a church or temple) is called a mosque. A Muslim worships the same god worshiped in Christianity and Judaism, but he calls God by the Arabic name Allah.

The mosque at Demak is the earliest known mosque on Java and is considered one of Indonesia's most important holy places for Muslims. Every Muslim in the country tries to make several journeys to worship at this mosque in Demak.

Constructed of wood, the structure has four main pillars in the central hall. One of them is said to be the pillar made by Sunan Kali Jogo. It is distinctive in that it is the only one that looks like it is made of pieces of wood glued together.

This story tells of the Wali Sanga, the nine wise men of Islam who were the first teachers of Islam in Java, and the mosque they built at Demak.

"Sunan" is a title originally given to a king on Java. It was later given to the holy men who brought Islam to Java.

The Widow and the Fishes

HERE was once a very old and very poor widow who lived by herself in a village on the island of Java. She was so poor she wore the same ragged *kain* and *kebaya* day after day, for, in truth, she owned just that one outfit. She had nothing to eat or drink except water. On good days, she had a small bowl of rice with her water. Because she had so little to eat, she dragged herself from one chore to another and always looked ill.

She looked forward to rice harvesting time when each worker received a share of the harvest every day. The old woman helped with the harvest and received her share, but the farmers were reluctant to give it to her, because she produced so little work.

At other times, she wandered around the forest and gathered sticks for firewood. These she traded with her wealthy neighbors for some rice. Her neighbors were self-centered and greedy and did nothing to help her.

During the rainy season, the shack she lived in could not keep the water out. Her roof was full of holes, and the sides were flimsy. One side leaned against her neighbor's wall, and her neighbor resented it.

Such was the widow's poverty, but added to this was her ignorance. Why, she had never even heard of Allah (God)!

On one of her hungry days, when she had nothing to eat, she walked slowly through the forest looking for firewood. She noticed the dry river bed with puddles of water here and there; the dry season had robbed the river of most of its water and its life. The sun was much too hot for the old woman, who had not eaten for the past two days. She could barely keep her feet going, but the thought of not eating again for yet another day kept her walking.

She hardly looked left or right, but a splash of color caught her eye. She stopped to look at the puddle of muddy water and saw a number of *gabus* fish packed closely together, struggling in the watery mud. They had been caught in a too-small puddle and were attempting to escape to a larger one. Now they were trapped by the dry river bed.

The old woman was beside herself with joy! She thought of all those fishes for dinner as she walked to the edge of the pool and leaned down. When she reached to scoop them up, she hesitated. The fish were all pressed together with their mouths turned up. Under the leadership of a big white fish, the *imam*, they were chanting, "Allah, ya, Allah! Send us rain! Give us rain or we will die!"

The fishes repeated this chant over and over again, their voices becoming louder and stronger as they chanted. Fascinated, the widow stepped back to the forest path and stood watching them. Time passed. The old woman continued to stand rooted to the spot. She was so captivated by the fishes that she did not see the dark clouds gather overhead. When the clouds burst and a torrential rainfall followed, the puddles, then the river bed, filled with water. After a while, the water flowed down the river to the lake in the valley below. The fishes swam away safely. The old woman stirred herself and walked slowly home. Forgotten were the sticks, her hunger, and her wet clothes.

How marvelous! she thought. The fishes asked for water and Allah gave them water. If the fishes can ask this someone they call Allah and have their prayer answered, why can't I do the same? Instead of water, I shall ask for money.

When she reached her humble shack, she had made up her mind. Sitting on the floor in the middle of her hut, she lost no time.

"Allah, ya, Allah! Send me coins! Give me money or I will die!"

She repeated this hour after hour, chanting in a loud voice, her faith in the goodness of Allah complete.

Her neighbor, of course, heard her and became annoyed. By

the second day, he was very angry. He ran to her house and yelled at her.

"Stop it!" he said. "You're driving me crazy with your shouting! Allah is not going to come and give you money, so stop it right now!"

The old woman ignored him completely, so intent was she in her praying. He stomped out and went back to his house, where he became angrier and angrier.

On the third day he lost all patience with the old woman. He stormed over to her house.

"Stop this nonsense!" he shouted. "You stupid woman! Allah will never give you money! Go out and gather sticks!"

The old woman continued with her chanting, as if he had not said a word. The neighbor went home in a fury and began to stuff a bag with bits of glass, stones, and shards of clay pots. That night, he climbed her roof and dropped the bag through a hole onto the sleeping woman. The bag hit the woman and knocked her unconscious for the rest of the night.

When she awoke the next morning, she saw the sack beside her. So absolute was her belief in Allah, she knelt and prayed in thanksgiving. "Thank you, Allah!" she said. "Now I will have something to eat every day." Then she opened the sack.

Silver and gold coins spilled out into her lap.

People heard of her wealth and came to visit her. Following the advice of the village head, the old widow moved to a home in the city where she was very comfortable. She was loved by all, because she never forgot her own poverty. The poor who came to her door were never turned away empty-handed.

When her neighbor heard of her good fortune, he was so jealous he began to scheme and plot. He felt that part of her wealth also belonged to him, because, wasn't the sack with its contents his?

He then hit upon an idea. If she can ask Allah for money, he thought, so can I.

The greedy man stuffed a bag with stones, shards of pottery, and broken glass, just what he had thrown on the old woman. As he tied the bag, he had *another* idea. Why not *two* bags? Then I shall have more money.

So he filled a second bag. Next, he instructed a servant to cut a hole in his roof and throw the two bags onto him on the third day. "If you do not do as I say," he warned, "you will lose your job here."

The man then sat comfortably in his room and began to chant just as the old woman had done. He wanted to be sure his actions and timing were exactly like hers.

"Allah, ya, Allah!" he shouted. "Send me coins! Give me money or I will die!" While he chanted, he kept thinking of the money he would have in a few days and how he would spend that money. The chant was no longer a prayer but just so many words. On the third night, his servant came quietly and cut a hole in the roof. Although he thought it all very strange, he remembered his master's warning and threw the two sacks down on him.

The first sack knocked the man unconscious, and the second broke his back.

When the man awoke, he was in a great deal of pain, but he eagerly opened the sacks. They contained the same rubble that he had placed in them! The man shrieked and cried in rage and disappointment.

Because of his back injury, he could no longer work. He became poorer and poorer until, in a few years, he became as poor as the old woman had been.

NOTES

This story points out how faith in Allah rewards a person. The old widow knew nothing of Allah except what her eyes and ears had witnessed. Yet, her faith was complete and absolute, while her neighbor, who knew of Allah, did not have faith. For his greed and lack of faith, he received a just reward.

In the Islamic religion, there is no formal priesthood. The *imam* leads the people in prayer and can be spokesman of the faith. Anyone can be an *imam*. But an *imam* cannot perform a funeral service; a *modin*, or village official, does. Neither can the *imam* perform weddings; a *naib*, or government official, does.

The *kain* is the skirt and the *kebaya*, the blouse. Details of attire are discussed under Clothing in More Notes on Indonesian Culture.

For information on rainfall and the dry season, see Climate under More Notes on Indonesian Culture.

The Story of Sangkuriang

NE day, long ago, when the district of Periangan was still covered with trees, in a time people called "a time of giants," Raden Sungging Perbangkara, a young aristocrat, entered the forest to hunt for game. He paused long enough to urinate on the large, flat, elephant-ear-shaped leaves of the *kladi* plant. His urine formed glistening puddles on each leaf. Soon, along came a wild pig looking for water to drink.

The shimmering liquid pools on the leaves caught the sow's eye, and she drank every drop, thinking it was water. Before too many days had gone by, the pig realized that she was going to have a baby. She thought back to the day the nobleman was in the forest when she had drunk the strangely salty water, and she knew whose child it was. Several moons later, the pig gave birth to a little girl.

The girl grew up in the forest until, one day, Raden Sungging Perbangkara happened to hunt in that part of the forest again. Astonished at seeing a child alone in the forest, he exclaimed, "Child, where are your parents? Are you lost in these woods?"

The pig, ever nearby, heard a man's voice and came to stand by her daughter. The sight of the wild pig recalled the nobleman to his hunt. He immediately raised his spear to kill the pig. The pig, in turn, saw that it was the same man whose urine she had drunk, causing her to have this daughter.

"Take this child," she said. "She is your daughter."

"Impossible!" the nobleman said. "I have never seen her before."

The pig explained how she had drunk his urine and had given birth to the girl.

Raden Sungging Perbangkara took the girl home to his palace and named her Dewi Rara Sati. She learned to spin and weave and loved to do this every day. Soon her fingers flew with the needle, so adept had she become.

One hot and humid day she decided to do her weaving on a shaded platform where she could capture the cool breezes above and below her. As the heat of the day slowed her fingers and lulled her senses, she dropped her thread. Feeling too lazy and lethargic to climb down to pick it up, she mumbled, "Will someone hand me my thread? I promise to make that woman my sister or, if it is a man, or even an animal, he will be my husband."

A dog came trotting by and picked up the thread for her. Wagging his tail, he jumped up on the platform and dropped the thread at her feet. Dewi Rara Sati was disappointed, but a promise was a promise, and she was afraid that if she did not keep her word, great misfortune would be her lot for the rest of her life. So she married the dog.

The day they were married, the dog spoke to Rara Sati. "Because of a spell placed on me, I must spend the rest of my life as a dog," he said. "But in human life I was a prince. Please call me Si Tumang."

A year later, Rara Sati gave birth to a handsome son. Si Tumang and Rara Sati named him Sangkuriang.

His mother never told him that Si Tumang was his father, but Sangkuriang felt very close to the dog and often felt that they were like brothers. From the day Sangkuriang could walk, Si Tumang accompanied him wherever he went.

When he became old enough to lift a spear, Sangkuriang began to go hunting with Si Tumang.

"When I kill an animal that is too large for me to carry home, I will bring only the flesh for you," he told his mother. "Is there any special part that I can also save for you?"

"Any part will do," his mother replied, "but I do like the liver."

So Sangkuriang and Si Tumang went hunting almost every day. Each time they went to the forest, they killed an animal and brought home its flesh and liver for his mother.

One day Sangkuriang was still empty-handed when darkness

crept up on them. He was reluctant to go home without anything for his mother, but try as he might, the game he stalked was elusive. Sorely troubled, he peered into the deepening darkness.

Just then he saw a wild pig, a most delicious-looking fat sow, run past him a short distance away. His first arrow missed the animal. When his second arrow wounded the big, fat pig, she screamed.

Quickly Sangkuriang ordered Si Tumang to track the pig and kill her, but the dog whined and did not move. Sangkuriang urged the dog to give chase, but Si Tumang refused to move because he knew that the sow was Sangkuriang's grandmother.

Si Tumang's disobedience angered Sangkuriang. In a fit of temper he turned on his dog and killed him. He cut off his head, sliced his flesh and carved out his liver to take home to his mother. Rara Sati did not question him, but cooked and ate the meat and liver. The next day she asked Sangkuriang, "Did you have a good hunt yesterday?"

"Yes," he answered.

"What was the animal you killed?"

Sangkuriang did not answer.

Rara Sati looked around and called, "Tumang! Si Tumang!" She looked puzzled. "How odd. Si Tumang is not here. Did he return with you last night?"

"Y-yes," Sangkuriang answered. His flesh and liver did return, he told himself.

Rara Sati looked closely at Sangkuriang. "Are you hiding something?" she asked. "Did something happen to Tumang?"

Sangkuriang did not know what to say. He did not know where to look. Overcome by a wave of anxiety and foreboding, Rara Sati's voice was unusually harsh as she asked, "Something happened to Si Tumang! What is it? What is it, Sangkuriang? Tell me!" She grabbed Sangkuriang by his shoulder and shook him.

Sangkuriang hung his head and told his mother of the barren hunt and how Tumang had disobeyed him, allowing a big fat sow to escape, causing him to lose his temper.

When she heard this, Rara Sati lost all control and, picking up a piece of cane, began to beat him on the head, saying, "How dare you! How dare you! Leave this house and never come back!"

She beat him so hard that she opened a wound on his head. She kept beating him so that blood flowed like water, and still she would not stop. Sangkuriang barely escaped with his life.

Years of wandering followed. Sangkuriang grew to be a handsome young man who had learned something about magic during this time.

As he walked through a forest one day, a forest like any other, he heard a woman singing. Her voice was sultry and inviting. He followed the sound of the voice and came upon a beautiful young woman washing her feet in the stream. He fell in love with her at once. He approached her and started a conversation. Hoping to make her his wife, he stayed at her side to get to know her better. She, too, fell in love with him.

They talked, they laughed, they rolled in the grass together in play, and she looked for lice in his hair when he laid his head in her lap.

"What is this scar you have on your scalp?" she asked.

"It's a scar from a beating my mother gave me," Sangkuriang answered. "I was still a boy when that happened."

The woman then knew that the man she had fallen in love with was Sangkuriang, her son. She was Dewi Rara Sati, whom the gods had given eternal youth.

She was reluctant to tell Sangkuriang that she was his mother. She refused to marry him, but Sangkuriang was insistent. He was determined to marry her.

She finally told Sangkuriang, "I cannot marry you. I am your mother."

"No, you are not!" he answered. "You are not my mother." He refused to believe her.

She decided, then, to impose an impossible condition.

"If you will make me a large lake and a boat for us to ride on that lake," she said, "I will marry you. But you must make them tonight and complete them before the cock crows at dawn tomorrow."

Sangkuriang agreed, confident that he could do it. In the years that he had wandered from place to place, he had become acquainted with forest nymphs and spirits. He called on them now for their magical assistance.

He worked hard all night, building a dam in the valley so that the water built up in the mountain, forming a lake where trees had once stood. Then he shaped and formed a gigantic boat to carry him and his wife on the lake. Shortly before dawn, the huge lake was finished and in place. Dewi Rara Sati saw that he would soon complete the boat and that she would have to marry him.

Now she used her own magical powers and created a ray of light on the horizon. She then took her red scarf and shook it at the cocks, waking them up. The cocks crowed.

Sangkuriang was so upset that he kicked the boat and his workbench, overturning both. Rara Sati flew to heaven, but Sangkuriang called to her, begging her to come back, promising to wait for her.

"Impossible!" Rara Sati said. "I cannot marry you—you who want to marry your mother and have killed your father."

"Come back!" Sangkuriang shouted. "I love you and will wait for you here!" He sat on a rock to wait, and wait, in vain.

NOTES

This is a well-known myth that is set in the area north of the Periangan district in Sunda on the island of Java.

The story explains the origin of the live crater Tangkuban Perahu, a prominent feature of the West Javanese landscape. The mountain is nearly 2,000 meters high, and its top is shaped like an inverted boat. Nearby is Bukit Tunggal, a hill that is said to be the overturned workbench. The lake that Sangkuriang created eventually dried up and became farming land. Not far from Tangkuban Perahu is Bandung, the third largest city of Indonesia.

Tangkuban Perahu means "upside-down boat."

The *kladi* plant is a type of taro.

"Raden" is a title meaning "king."

The Palace at Solo

A king living in a very old palace in Kartasura just west of Surakarta in Central Java long, long ago wanted to move to "somewhere better," but he had no idea where that was. After thinking of different ways to find that "better" place, he chose to let an elephant decide.

An elephant was let loose in the palace courtyard. The elephant wandered around the courtyard before going out of the palace grounds. Wherever it went, the king and his family followed.

The elephant first stopped in the village of Kadipolo in Surakarta, so the king settled there and ordered his people to build a new palace in that village. While the people were working on the palace, the elephant started to walk again, leaving Kadipolo and stopping at a place called Solo, still within the region of Surakarta. So the king halted work on the palace at Kadipolo, although it was partly built, and ordered everyone to Solo (Sala).

There in Solo, which is the name people use for Surakarta, the king met an Islamic teacher called Kyai Sala, who asked the elephant, "Why are you resting here?" The elephant did not answer.

The king replied, "We are going to build a new palace, because this is where the elephant stopped."

"But," Kyai Sala said, "why are you building a big palace here on ground that is as wet and sandy as this?"

"As long as Kyai Sala lives here," the king replied, "we can build a new palace without any problem, because you will protect it."

The next day, construction of the new palace began. Surakarta Palace, a big and beautiful structure, was built to completion. The ground, which was wet and sandy as Kyai Sala had said, became drier every year after the palace was completed. The king, who gained the title Paku Buwono I, was the first to live in Surakarta Palace.

Paku Buwono's descendants continued to live in that palace, even to this day.

NOTES

Kadipolo is in Surakarta. Solo, or Sala, is today another name for Surakarta. At one time, it was said to be full of swampland because of the water seeping in from the Bengawan Solo River. Although the ground under Surakarta Palace has been improving every year, occasionally the city suffers a bad flood. Once in the 1960s floodwaters reached about two meters high.

Elephants often represent Ganesha, Hindu god and son of Shiva, because he had an elephant's head on a human body. Ganesha is known today as the Hindu god of knowledge and the guide of everyone.

Because there is no one accepted version of how the Sunan's Palace in Surakarta came to be, this story is just one of many told by the people.

For information on rainfall, see Climate under More Notes on Indonesian Culture.

The Legendary Jaka Tarub

ONG, long ago in the primeval times of Java, there lived a man by the name of Kyai ageng ing-Kudus whose youngest son, Ki Jaka, refused to marry when he came of age. Knowing that he had upset his father, Ki Jaka left home one night and walked until he reached the mountain called Kendeng, where he practiced asceticism, a form of worship that caused him to turn away from the comforts of life. As the days went by, he wandered farther into the dense growth of the mountain until he came upon a peaceful spot by a pool with flowering trees overhanging the water.

He sat there to meditate, not knowing that this garden was owned by Kyai ageng Kembang-Lampir, whose beautiful daughter had, also, refused to marry. While Ki Jaka was there, she came to fill her water jug and bathe in the pool. She was so beautiful that he found he did want to marry and tried to persuade her.

After a time, the daughter of Kyai ageng Kembang-Lampir found she was with child, but her father did not know who the child's father was, and she would not reveal his name. He was so angry that she ran away one night and had her baby in the forest alone. She died in childbirth, but her son lived.

A hunter in pursuit of a doe saw the baby and picked him up and carried him on the hunt. Then, all of a sudden, the hunter lost sight of the doe, and so he put the baby down to look for his prey.

The spot where he laid the baby down was the hermitage of Tarub village, where Kyai ageng ing-Tarub, a much respected religious man, had lived. The widow of Kyai ageng ing-Tarub, who still lived there, found the baby and adopted him, calling him Jaka.

As he grew up, Jaka Tarub's favorite pastime was hunting with his blowpipe. He became quite an accomplished hunter as a young man.

One day, as he walked through the forest looking high up into the trees, he sighted a strange and beautiful bird. Before he could shoot it, the bird flew away into the dense growth of trees and vines. Jaka Tarub followed it.

As the forest path passed under a thick canopy of leaves and branches, the bird alighted on a tree. But Jaka Tarub was no longer interested in the bird. His eyes were drawn to a ray of sunlight streaking through the growth of trees. That ray of light appeared to carry women's laughter. He peered around the trunk of a tree and saw a beautiful lake with clear, quiet waters, with several maidens splashing and playing in it.

So beautiful were these maidens and so surprised was Jaka Tarub that he was struck dumb for the longest while. He hid behind a tree and discovered where the angels, as he had assumed they were, had thrown off their clothes carelessly. He took one of the garments and hid it.

Soon the angels left the water and picked up their clothes. They dressed and together prepared to fly back to heaven. But one angel could not find her jacket that would lift her back to heaven. She looked in the bushes, in the trees, and under the floor of forest leaves. She was terribly upset, especially when her sister angels prepared to leave for home. She looked frantically for her jacket, but to no avail. She sat down and cried as her sisters flew away.

Soon after the last angel had left, Jaka Tarub came out of hiding and approached the remaining angel.

"Beautiful maiden, why are you crying?" he asked.

"I cannot find my jacket, and I cannot go home without it," she replied in a sad voice.

"Here is an extra shirt I always carry with me," he said. "Wear it until I take you home to my mother. Her clothes will fit you better than this."

Jaka Tarub took the beautiful angel home, and she stayed with him and his mother. Her name was Dewi Nawang Wulan.

Not long after that, Nawang Wulan and Jaka Tarub were married. The widow of Tarub was overjoyed. Although Nawang Wulan thought of her heavenly home often, she was happy with her husband. Within a year, Jaka Tarub and Nawang Wulan had a daughter, Rara Nawang Sih.

The family prospered. There was always enough to eat, and their rice supply never seemed to lessen. When the widow of Tarub died, Jaka Tarub adopted the name of Kyai ageng ing-Tarub.

One day, while Nawang Wulan was cooking rice, she had to go to the river to wash some of the baby's clothes. Asking her husband to watch the rice until it was done and warning him repeatedly not to open the pot in her absence, she hurried away.

Jaka Tarub was curious. He decided that a little peek into the rice pot was harmless, so he lifted the cover. He was surprised to see just one stalk of rice in the pot. Now he knew why they never ran out of rice, but, by lifting the pot cover, he had unknowingly broken Nawang Wulan's magic spell.

When Nawang Wulan came home, she could not understand why the rice did not cook. She finally guessed that her husband had opened the pot.

"My dear husband," she said, greatly upset, "you will be sorry for what you've done. Our rice supply will be eaten up very quickly, and we will have to pound the rice stalk."

And so it happened that Nawang Wulan went to the rice shed one day to pound the rice stalk to separate the grain from the plant. As she scraped the floor to gather the stalks, she caught sight of a fragment of yellow cloth beneath a stack of straw covering the floor. She pulled on it and found her lost jacket, the magical jacket named Onta Kusuma, which Jaka Tarub had taken at the pond. She quickly put it on and felt her supernatural powers return. She prepared to go home to heaven. She left a message for her husband, asking him to burn the rice straw of black glutinous rice whenever he needed her. She in heaven would then return to earth to care for Nawang Sih. Then, wearing the jacket Onta Kusuma, Nawang Wulan ascended to heaven on the smoke of the burning rice straw and black glutinous rice.

Nawang Wulan kept her promise and came down to earth to feed and care for her daughter whenever her husband called.

Nawang Sih thrived and grew up to look like her mother. Kyai ageng ing-Tarub continued to live a quiet life there in the forest, forever sorry that he had lifted the rice pot cover.

NOTES

It is said that Nawang Sih became the ancestress of the house of Mataram. Mataram was a large kingdom in Java and one of the longest-ruling dynasties in Javanese history. The first king of Mataram, Senapati, tried in vain to unite the whole island of Java, but not until 1613, when Sultan Agung was on the throne, did most of Java come under the house of Mataram.

Jaka Tarub himself is a well-known legendary figure to the Javanese in Central Java. He is often depicted in paintings and batiks in which incidents from his story are repeated. The story as a whole has been frequently told and performed as drama set to music as well as dance.

This myth is believed to be one of the most important and best known of the Javanese tales.

Nawang Wulan's jacket has no name in many versions of this tale. Some versions name the jacket because it has the miraculous power to lift a person from earth to heaven.

Out of Harm's Way

PAK Karto and his wife Ibu Karto lived in the forest far from any village. As much as they wanted children, their long marriage had not produced any.

One day, Ibu Karto had an idea. "Why don't we look for a banyan tree? If we pray for a child by the tree, God may answer our prayer."

"It is worth a try," her husband answered. "But we must look in the forest for such a tree. There is none around these parts."

The next day they set out into the dense forest surrounding their home. They walked for a long time before they came to a big banyan tree with a thick trunk and a rock under it, just the kind of tree they were looking for. With legs crossed in front of them, they sat facing the tree and prayed fervently for a child. While they were praying, a huge giant appeared and towered over them.

"Don't be afraid," he said. "I am here to grant you your wish."

The couple were overjoyed. "Wise Giant," they said, "we wish so much to have a child. We've been married for a long time but have no children."

"I will grant your wish," the giant replied, "on one condition. If the child is a boy, you may keep him forever. If it is a girl, you must give her to me after she is grown. Give me your promise on this."

The couple could not answer for a while, so astonished were they at the giant's condition. They finally decided to accept his offer.

"Good," the giant said. "Go home now. You will have the child you want." He disappeared, leaving two very happy people.

The couple waited anxiously for the baby to come. In just a few months, a beautiful baby girl was born to them. The baby brought great happiness to the couple, but the thought of the giant cast a shadow over their hearts.

The child was named Timun Mas. She was a well-behaved and loving child. As she grew, her beauty also grew. Whenever she looked at her daughter, the mother felt the giant's presence. The thought of losing their daughter saddened both parents so much that, one day, Timun Mas asked, "Why are you so sad all day?"

"It's nothing," they said. "Nothing that you need to worry about."

One morning Ibu Karto looked out her door, and there was the giant, standing at the edge of the forest.

"What do you have?" he asked. "A boy or a girl?"

Sadly, they answered, "A girl. Please, Wise Giant, please let us keep her for a while longer. We do really love her and will miss her terribly when she leaves."

"All right," the giant answered. "I'll come at the next full moon. Be sure you have her ready to go with me then."

"Thank you," both said, "thank you, Wise Giant." When he was gone, both parents were very sad. They had grown so attached to Timun Mas that it was impossible to think of letting her go.

At the next full moon, the giant returned to the house in the woods to claim Timun Mas.

"Where is Timun Mas?" he asked. "Is she ready to go with me?"

"Wait just a few minutes while she gets ready," her father said, determined to keep the giant occupied while Ibu Karto ran to the back of the house where Timun Mas was picking flowers.

"My love," her mother said in an urgent whisper, "you must run away to the forest. Do not worry about your father and me. The giant has come for you, and you must save yourself from him. Take this package with you. It contains cucumber seeds, a needle, shrimp paste, and salt. When trouble threatens, throw these items to the ground one by one." Then she gave Timun Mas a last hug and turned her in the direction of the forest.

Timun Mas ran into the forest as fast as she could while her mother returned to the giant.

"Where is Timun Mas?" he asked again.

"She is gone," her mother answered.

"Well," the giant said, "no matter how fast she runs, I can catch her." He started to run after Timun Mas. She ran as fast as she could, but the giant was soon very close behind her. Just as she expected to feel his hand on her shoulder, she remembered the package and the instructions her mother had given her.

Scooping up the cucumber seeds, she threw them on the ground behind her. Instantly, the magic seeds grew into a garden full of luscious, juicy cucumbers. The giant, who was reaching out to grab Timun Mas, stopped in his tracks. He loved cucumbers!

While he ate them, Timun Mas put as much distance as she could between them.

When the giant had his fill of cucumbers, he realized that Timun Mas was far away. He got up and began to run after her.

In the meantime, Timun Mas was so tired and breathless from running fast and far that she began to slow down. She saw that the giant was getting closer. She remembered the needle in the package. She threw it to the ground and almost at once a bamboo forest sprang up. The thick bamboo forest hid many sharp-stemmed branches.

The giant was trapped inside. While he struggled to get out, the sharp stems cut his skin, causing many bleeding cuts. When he finally escaped from the bamboo, he was so angry, he ran faster than ever.

Timun Mas was frightened when she saw how fast he ran and how angry he looked. She threw the next item to the ground—salt.

The salt caused a great, deep ocean to appear. In order to catch Timun Mas, the giant had to swim across the ocean. The cuts on the giant's skin smarted in the saltwater, and the giant became even angrier!

As he pulled himself from the ocean, he shouted to Timun Mas, "No matter what you do, Timun Mas, I can catch you, you know. Understand that I will have you."

Again the giant drew closer to Timun Mas in his chase. She remembered the last thing that her mother had given her, the shrimp paste. She threw that on the ground and was away just as the paste turned into a deep mud ocean.

While Timun Mas ran, the giant struggled in the mud. This time he could not get out, and he drowned.

Timun Mas was finally free of the giant, but she was lost in the large forest. She had been so frightened of the giant she had run without looking at the trail. She wanted to go home to her parents but did not know which way to turn. She was lost, and all alone. She tried to make a shelter under the trees.

Meanwhile, not far away, there was a place called Jenggolo where King Putro reigned. The king often went hunting with his soldiers and commanders.

One day they hunted for hours in the forest and had nothing, not even a deer, to show for their efforts. Discouraged, King Putro was ready to order his men back to Jenggolo when he caught sight of a young girl with a fair face, wearing a torn dress.

"Young woman!" King Putro said. "What is your name? Where are you from? And what are you doing here?"

"I am Timun Mas," she replied. "My father is Karto. He lives in the forest far from any village. The closest is Jenggolo."

"Why are you so far from home, then?"

"I was chased by a giant," she replied.

"Where is that giant now?" he asked.

"He perished in the shrimp paste mud," Timun Mas replied. "Now that he is dead, will Your Majesty please help me find my way home?"

"Very well," he replied. "Follow me and my men."

They picked their way through the forest and came to the palace. King Putro ordered the palace servants to bathe Timun Mas and dress her in fine dresses. When Timun Mas was clean and dressed, she was beautiful! The king looked at her in some astonishment because she looked as beautiful as an angel.

King Putro fell in love with Timun Mas.

"Timun Mas," he said, "will you be my queen?"

To his surprise and consternation, she said not a word but bent her head and cried.

"Why are you crying?" the astonished king asked.

"I cannot accept your proposal," Timun Mas replied. "I am not of royal blood, and my parents are humble people. I am not fit to be your queen."

"It does not matter to me, Timun Mas," the king replied gently. "To me, you are more beautiful than an angel. And you are as good and kind as one. What really matters is, do you love me? Please think this over for a few days before you give me your answer."

Timun Mas, who had loved the king from the moment she first laid eyes on him, joyfully agreed to become his queen. The wedding party that joined the king and Timun Mas in marriage included her parents and everybody in Jenggolo. It was a most happy gathering for everyone.

NOTES

According to the belief of certain Indonesians, the banyan tree holds a holy force and the rock under it is considered sacred. The position the couple used when praying, with legs crossed in front of them, is the traditional Indonesian praying position.

Parental love is an important aspect of life in Indonesia. The strength of this love is often a primary concern of stories in Indonesian folklore. In this story of Timun Mas, in which a beautiful child is given to aging parents who cannot give her up when the time comes, the love of the parents for their daughter is clear.

Some folklorists have compared the long chase of Timun Mas by the giant to a virtuous life constantly threatened by evil.

How Rice Came to Earth (1)

ONCE long ago, Lord Guru, head of all the gods in heaven, decided to build a new meetinghouse. He gathered all the lesser gods and asked for their help in supplying building materials and labor.

Each god had a specific assignment. One was asked to bring wood, another was asked to bring sand, still another was asked to bring tiles, and so on until everyone had something to bring and a task to do. The gods were excited to be a part of this project and began to bustle about gathering the materials they needed.

The god Narada looked around at the activity and saw all his friends except one, the god Anta. He visited Anta at home and found his friend's snakelike body coiled in a corner. Anta himself looked sad and morose.

"Why are you sitting here? Why aren't you getting supplies for the new meetinghouse? And why aren't you helping?" Narada asked.

"I would like so much to help," Anta answered, "but, you know, my body is not shaped like yours, and I have no arms or legs." And Anta shed three tears.

As the three tears touched the ground, they turned into three eggs before the eyes of the astonished gods.

"Oh, this is a good sign," Narada said. "Take these eggs as gifts to Lord Guru. At the same time, explain to him why you cannot help with the building."

"Of course," Anta said. "That is an excellent suggestion. Thank you, my dear friend." For the first time since Narada came, he smiled. He picked up each egg in his mouth.

As his body skimmed the ground slowly with the three eggs held ever so carefully, Anta set off for Lord Guru's palace. He was concentrating so hard on avoiding any jarring movements that he did not hear the flap of wings above him. He was startled to hear a voice greet him.

"Good day to you, dear friend Anta."

Anta looked up and saw his friend the garuda bird. With a mouthful of eggs, Anta could not answer.

"I say, dear friend Anta, this is a beautiful day. Where are you off to?"

Anta still did not reply.

"Friend Anta, did you not hear me?"

When there was still no response, the garuda bird began to ruffle its feathers. Anta could tell that he was becoming annoyed.

"God Anta, surely you can hear. Why do you ignore me?"

After receiving no answer again, the garuda bird flapped its wings and brushed Anta's body.

"I said, 'Good day,' Anta."

When his sixth greeting still brought forth no response, the garuda bird was highly insulted and very angry. He attacked Anta with his beak and sharp claws. In agony, Anta cried out. Two eggs rolled out of his mouth and shattered on a rock. A wild pig ran out of each egg.

Wounded and bleeding, Anta finally reached the palace and placed the remaining egg before Lord Guru. He explained why he could not help with the building and related his experience of that day.

"Of course, I understand your particular situation," Lord Guru assured Anta. "You do not have to assist with the meetinghouse. But I do appreciate this egg. Will you take it home and care for it until it hatches? Then bring it back to me."

Anta very happily took the egg home and tended it. Within several days, it hatched and produced a beautiful baby girl. Lord Guru was very pleased and instructed his wife to feed the baby with her own milk and to raise the child as one of their own. The baby was named Nji Pohatji Sang-Hyang Sri Dang-Yang Tisnawati. Everyone affectionately called her Sang-Hyang Sri. She grew into a charming and beautiful young woman whom everyone loved. Eventually, her charms also ensnared Lord

Guru's interest. He fell in love with her and wanted to marry her.

When he set the wedding date, the other gods were horrified because Guru would break a law of heaven by marrying his own child. They were afraid that disaster would befall all of them. But no amount of pleading and arguing shook Guru in his resolve to wed Sang-Hyang Sri. The gods were in a predicament. They met many times to discuss this problem before they came to the unhappy conclusion that Sang-Hyang Sri had to die. They offered a poison to the unsuspecting princess. She died immediately.

The princess' death caused deep sorrow. Several days after she was buried, a coconut tree grew from the spot where her head lay, rice plants from the vicinity of her eyes, and trees and grasses from other parts of her body. Every plant that grew from her body was strange and new to the people, but they discovered that each provided food and sustenance.

In time, the rice plant became the most cultivated plant, and its grain became the staple food for all of Java.

NOTES

Rice is the staple food of most of the people of Indonesia. Because of its importance, many stories explaining its origin exist in the Indonesian archipelago. Almost all of the tales have a common element—the rice seed or plant comes from the gods. Dewi Sri is the goddess most often associated by the Javanese with the rice harvest.

See "How Rice Came to Earth (2)" for the Sulawesi version.

The garuda bird is a mythological bird that has its origins in Hindu mythology. Indian art pictures the bird with the head, wings, talons, and back of an eagle and the body and limbs of a man. It is the official symbol of modern Indonesia.

"Dewi" is a title meaning "princess."

Bali

Creation of the Bali Channel

A long time ago in East Java, there lived a kind and holy man by the name of Sidi Mantri. He was a devout man and prayed to his god Shiva every day. His devotion did not go unnoticed by Shiva, who gave him a beautiful wife and a comfortable fortune over the years.

As grateful as he was to Shiva, Sidi Mantri was not happy. He did not have a son. Because he had no child, he was known as Empu Bekung, "childless master." Every day he prayed to the gods for a son who would be able to help him in his old age and fill his life from day to day.

At long last Shiva granted him this wish, and Sidi Mantri had a son. What rejoicing! He named the baby Manik Angkeran. The baby was strong and healthy and grew up very fast. Sidi Mantri doted on his only child.

But by the time Manik Angkeran reached young manhood, he had developed some very bad faults. One was that he was lazy. He did not help his aging father.

"Manik Angkeran," his father would say, "I need your help in the next village. Shall we start off early in the morning?"

"Father," he would answer, "I promised to meet my friends in the morning. I cannot help you."

Sidi Mantri excused his son and did without his assistance. But what was so important about meeting his friends? Manik Angkeran's second fault was gambling. He never won, but he cared not because his father took care of his gambling debts. If his father did not, he borrowed from friends.

Very soon his father's fortune dwindled to nothing. Sidi

Mantri prayed to Shiva to make his son a better person. Shiva appeared to him in a dream.

"There is a large deposit of gold and diamonds in the mountain Agung east of your home," he said. "The treasure is guarded by the dragon Besakih. Tell him I sent you. He will help you replenish your depleted wealth."

When he awoke, Sidi Mantri decided to seek Besakih and the treasure he guarded. He walked up the side of Gunung Agung. Just as he reached the top of the ridge, he came face to face with Besakih.

"What do you want?" Besakih asked in a threatening voice.

"The god Shiva sent me," Sidi Mantri answered. "All that I own I have sold or used to pay my son's gambling debts, and still there are more to take care of. Shiva said you would help me."

Besakih knew of the holiness and great kindness of Sidi Mantri, and he was only too happy to give him much gold and diamonds. Sidi Mantri was able to pay all of his son's debts with the treasure Besakih gave him.

But Manik Angkeran did not change. He continued his heedless ways until he was again knee-deep in new debts.

"Manik Angkeran," his father said, "how are we going to pay your debts? We have used up everything that the god Shiva gave us."

"You said that Besakih guards a huge store," Manik Angkeran said. "Go back and ask for more!"

Sidi Mantri could not pay these new debts, so he again, reluctantly, went to Gunung Agung to seek the dragon Besakih's help.

When he climbed to the top of Gunung Agung, Besakih was surprised to see him.

"What brings you here so soon after your last visit?" he asked.

"I come for the same reason," Sidi Mantri replied. "My son has not learned yet and has made new gambling debts."

"I shall give you enough, but this is the last time," Besakih said. "Do not return to ask me again."

Upon arriving home, Sidi Mantri gave the precious stones to his son with these words. "This is the last time I can ask for help. Do not create any more gambling debts."

"Where do you get these precious stones?" Manik Angkeran

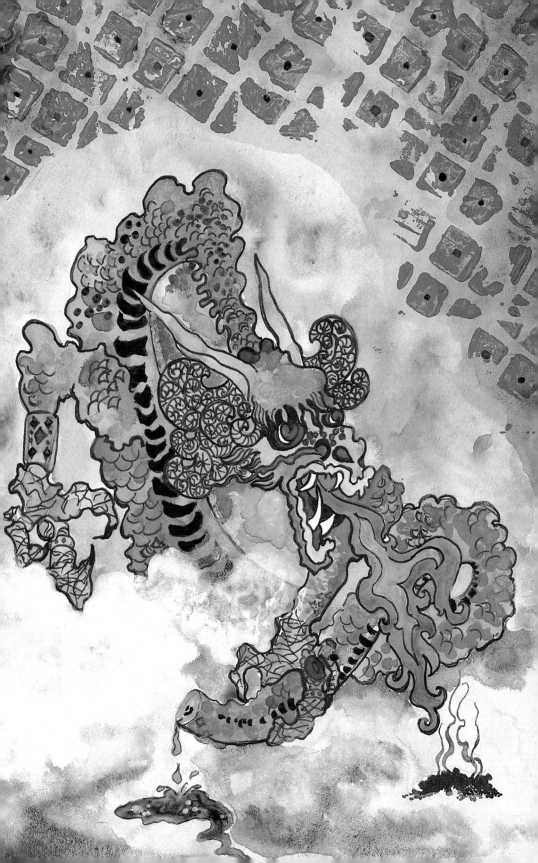

asked his father. "If I could go instead, I would not have to bother you any more."

"It does not matter where I get these, because we may not depend on them any more," his father said and refused to discuss the source of this fortune.

Manik Angkeran then asked various friends and, through them, discovered where to go. Early the following morning, while his father slept, he went to Gunung Agung. There he met the dragon Besakih, who asked him who he was and what he wanted. Manik Angkeran told the dragon of his troubles and asked the dragon to help him with gold and diamonds. The dragon Besakih said, "If you promise not to gamble any more and become a good man, I shall give you all the gold and diamonds you need to clear your debts."

"Oh, yes, I promise," Manik Angkeran said.

Then the dragon Besakih turned to go into the mountain to bring him the gold and diamonds. As he turned, Manik Angkeran saw that the dragon's tail sparkled with a ring of gold, diamonds, and precious gems. Quickly he drew his *kris* and cut Besakih's tail and ran away with it as fast as he could. But the dragon breathed fire on him, reducing him to ashes.

In the meantime, Sidi Mantri awoke and could not find his son. He waited, but Manik Angkeran did not come.

Sidi Mantri, by inquiring in the village, concluded that his son had gone to seek out the dragon Besakih. He then walked to Gunung Agung to see Besakih.

"If you can give me back my tail, I will bring Manik Angkeran back to life. But he will have to be punished," Besakih said. "His punishment is that he must live with me in the mountain."

Sidi Mantri was happy to know that his son would have life again. He went in search of the dragon's tail. After several days of walking and looking, he found the tail and carried it back to Besakih. He repaired the tail so that Besakih had his full tail again. Only then did the dragon bring Manik Angkeran back to life.

Bidding his son a sad farewell, Sidi Mantri started on his way home. As soon as he left Gunung Agung behind him, Sidi Mantri began to strike the ground with his cane. He pounded and pounded with all his strength until water started to spurt out of the ground. More and more water came out until there was an ocean of water. Sidi Mantri had created an ocean to separate his homeland from Gunung Agung so that his son could not return to East Java to gamble any more.

Sidi Mantri lived out his days in East Java, again known by his former name, Empu Bekung, childless master.

NOTES

This story tells how Manik Angkeran disregards the basic Indonesian practices of reverence for the aged and of mutual assistance or working together (*gotong royong*). Manik Angkeran is punished by Shiva for his disregard for his aged parents, his self-centered ways, and his lazy and greedy habits. The Bali Channel forever separated him from Java, Manik Angkeran's homeland.

It is said that Mount Agung at one time rose up to the clouds at the eastern end of Java Island. Since the days of Manik Angkeran, it has been located on Bali Island, separated from East Java by the Bali Channel.

"Gunung" means mountain or mount.

The Tragedy of Jayaprana

O n Bali Island once, long ago, a terrible epidemic swept through a village. Many people died, including the parents and two sisters of Jayaprana.

Jayaprana was still a little boy when he was left an orphan. Since there were so many deaths from this plague, the king himself came to visit the *kampung,* or village, in order to cheer the survivors. He saw Jayaprana, a handsome and polite youngster, and took a liking to him. He decided to take Jayaprana home and raise him in the palace.

Jayaprana grew up to be a favored employee of the king. When he reached the age of twenty-five, the king suggested that he choose a bride. Jayaprana refused at first, but he met Ni Layonsari, older daughter of Jero Bandesa, head of the Banjar Sekar village, and he wanted to marry her.

The king was pleased and built a house for the young couple. He also planned a festive wedding party for Jayaprana.

On the day of the wedding, Ni Layonsari wore a beautiful wedding gown with jewelry of pure gold. She rode in a golden litter carried by six men, while Jayaprana rode a handsome black horse.

This wedding day was the day the king first saw the bride. She was so beautiful that he fell in love with her. He wanted to cancel the wedding and claim the bride for himself. One of his soldiers, whose name was I Sawunggaling, stopped him.

"Wait until the party is over, Your Majesty," he said. "There are too many people coming to the wedding party. I shall think of a way to fool him."

During the feasting, the king's wives knew that he was eyeing the bride, and they were jealous of her. But Jayaprana and his bride were blissfully unaware of the king's plans.

The king waited until the wedding was over before he called his personal guards. "I want him destroyed," he said. "I want him out of the way so I can marry his wife."

I Sawunggaling said, "I've thought of a plan to fool him, Your Majesty. I'll take him to the west, to Terima Gulf, where many people have been captured by foreigners and tortured. The foreigners stole the people's cattle and killed the villagers."

"Good!" the king said. "Then you will take care of this matter for me."

Three days after the wedding, the impatient king sent for Jayaprana.

"Go to Terima Gulf," he said. "A small group of foreign soldiers has landed and is causing some trouble there. You will have forty soldiers with you."

Jayaprana did not question the king's order and prepared to leave in the morning. Ni Layonsari cried and begged him to stay with her. They had an extremely happy marriage, and parting even for a few weeks was very difficult for both.

On his way to Terima Gulf, Jayaprana experienced many problems caused by I Sawunggaling, but day after day, they encountered no enemy and no report of any hostility. He began to suspect that he had been fooled by the king. He then suspected, also, that the king wanted him out of the way for a reason.

On their first night at Terima Gulf, while Jayaprana slept, I Sawunggaling stabbed Jayaprana repeatedly with his *kris* until he died.

Jayaprana's face in death was almost a smile, as if he were having pleasant dreams in his sleep. The blood that spilled smelled fragrant. The soldiers who witnessed this crime cried, knowing that the killing had been for no good reason.

They buried Jayaprana and started on their way home. Suddenly, out of nowhere, forty tigers attacked them and killed many of the soldiers. Thunder and lightning appeared from a clear sky. Trees toppled on the men. Farther on, a number of them were bitten by snakes and died. Only ten survived to reach the palace.

They reported to the king. He beat his chest and cried,

"Jayaprana! No! So young to leave us!" He made a great show of his grief.

Meanwhile, Ni Layonsari asked the soldiers about her husband. None of them wanted to tell her the truth. Finally, one of them, feeling sorry for her, told her that he had been killed by the king's order.

Ni Layonsari's grief was so great she wanted to die also. She fainted, and in a swoon, she saw her husband's shadow standing in front of her.

"Sari, my lovely wife," he cried, "we had to bid each other farewell after such a short time together. If the king summons you, be careful. Take care of yourself. I shall wait for you in heaven forever."

He disappeared, leaving his wife in a fresh flood of tears.

The next day she did receive a summons to the palace. The king tried to console her and, at the same time, attempted to win her for himself. But he failed. Hating the king, Ni Layonsari could stand no more of him. Grabbing the king's *kris*, she stabbed herself and died. The king, bewildered by what had happened, hugged her and babbled on to her as if he were out of his mind. When he finally realized that she was dead, he became angry and stormed out of the palace and killed several people before he killed himself.

The story of this unfortunate event reached the ears of some of the king's loyal soldiers. They thought that the people were responsible for the death of their ruler, and so they went to the village to avenge his death. Friend no longer knew friend. Before the day ended, the palace and the village were destroyed. Only the family of Jero Bandesa survived to live peacefully.

Ni Layonsari and I Jayaprana, it was believed, were together again in heaven.

NOTES

The Balinese believe that the murder of an innocent person is a crime that will eventually be avenged on the murderer and the murderer's family. Because of the murder of innocent Jayaprana, animals attacked the soldiers, the weather turned bad, and trees fell on them. Then the king went out of his mind and killed himself.

The *kris* is a type of dagger that is especially significant in

Javanese and Balinese culture. For additional information on the *kris,* turn to More Notes on Indonesian Culture.

"I" before a name indicates that the person named is male, whereas "Ni" indicates female. This is a common practice in Bali.

Early Indonesian kings were believed to have divine powers in their lifetime. This allowed them to have many privileges, such as having as many wives as they wished.

Kalimantan

Why We Have Insects, Bees, and Birds

ENAI and Manang were a happily married couple. They were so happy that Dia, a wicked old witch, was jealous of Jenai and plotted to get rid of her.

One day, when Manang was not around, Dia called on Jenai at her home in the forest.

"Let us go to the stream to take a bath and fish," she said.

"No," Jenai said. "I don't care to go today."

Dia was persistent. The day was very warm and the thought of serving fish to Manang finally persuaded Jenai to go with Dia.

They walked to the stream and picked a shady spot where trees arched overhead and roots clung to the earth and water. Smooth pebbles of different sizes lined the stream bed, and the water was clear and deep. After their bath, they began to fish. While Jenai was intent on drawing in her line, Dia picked up a dead branch from the ground and whacked her on the head. Jenai slumped over into the water, and Dia pushed her body down among the roots of the trees. Then Dia changed her own form to that of Jenai. Although she looked exactly like Jenai, her voice remained hoarse. It was not the sweet and gentle voice of Jenai.

When Manang came home from the hunt, he noticed nothing different except her voice. Thinking that his wife had a sore throat, he did not mention it. After several months, however, he began to wonder.

"Jenai," he said one day, "your voice used to be so sweet, but now it's strange and harsh. Do you still have a sore throat?"

"I don't think I can ever get rid of it," Dia answered. "I dreamed about an old woman who wants me to make offerings to her to cure my throat."

"Well, then," Manang said, "make the offerings." And he said no more about her voice.

Jenai, meanwhile, appeared to her mother in a dream. She told her mother exactly where in the stream her body was lodged and asked her to retrieve it. If she would make an offering to the gods, Jenai would also be able to live again. Her mother did everything that Jenai asked, and Jenai lived. Not knowing what to do about Dia, Jenai decided to stay with her mother for a while.

Sometime after this, Manang visited his mother-in-law and saw Jenai there. She told him everything that had happened and how Dia had tricked both of them. When he left Jenai, he was full of hatred for Dia and planned his revenge carefully.

Behaving as if everything were normal, he said, "Your throat is still not well. Let us make an offering to the gods." Dia agreed.

They went to the forest to look for bamboos in which to store the cooked rice. When they saw a bamboo grove, Manang said, "Hold this end of the bamboo for me while I cut it to the right length."

Dia held the bamboo while Manang started to cut it, closer and closer to her hands. "Be careful, or you'll cut my hands," she said.

"Of course, I see your hands," he said. "I'm not as blind as you think."

As he kept cutting, he suddenly struck her, cutting her hands, then her legs, and then her body.

As her body was cut into small pieces, she cursed him. "May every piece of my flesh turn into insects, bees, and birds that will threaten your children and your children's children through the years that are coming. The insects and bees will sting them and the birds will ruin their crops."

Even as she cursed him, her flesh turned into insects, birds, and bees, just as she had said. Mosquitoes swarmed over Manang, and he had to fight them off as he walked home.

Now that they were free of Dia, Jenai and Manang had a very happy life together. But the world since then has never been free of insects, birds, and bees.

This story of why we have insects, birds, and bees comes from the Dayak people of the island of Borneo. The Indonesian part of Borneo is called Kalimantan. (See the endpapers.)

"Dayak" is a name given to the indigenous people of the island, people who were already living there long before the first recorded settlers came.

The Dayaks living in the interior and in the mountain regions are known as Land Dayaks, and those living along the coast are known as Sea Dayaks.

No Tigers in Borneo

NCE, long ago in the jungles of Java, tigers found less and less food to eat. The Raja of All Tigers knew his followers would soon starve. Calling his minister to his side, he discussed this problem with him. Finally he growled, "I have decided. Go to the forests of Borneo. Tell the Raja of Borneo that he must send me food every month. If he should refuse, we attack in seven days, and we will have a war." He growled deep in his throat, then pulled a whisker from his face. "Take this whisker to him. This will show him how big and strong I am, and he will not refuse!" Then the Raja of All Tigers roared his challenge to the Raja of Borneo, and the minister quaked in his tiger's stripes.

That night, three tigers left the jungles of Java and swam across the Java Sea to Borneo. Before they entered the forest there, all three together gave a terrible roar to announce their arrival. Not a sound nor a movement in the forest greeted them.

The three tigers stepped into the tangle of trees and padded on soundless feet, looking for the Raja of Borneo. They looked to the east, they looked to the west. They went north and they went south. The forest was still. All the animals had heard their roar and had run to hide. The three tigers walked so quietly that one little animal, the tiny mouse-deer, did not hear them approaching. Curious to see if the danger had passed, he poked his head out of the shelter of fallen logs and jumped when the minister snarled over his shoulder, "Where is the Raja of Borneo? I bring a message to him from the Raja of All Tigers of Java."

Kancil, the mouse-deer, looked at the three tigers and felt his whole body quiver like jelly. With a great effort, he hid his feel-

ings from the three pairs of eyes riveted on him. He thought quickly and, in a voice much like his everyday voice, answered, "The Raja of Borneo is hunting in the northern forest today," and he bowed to them. "I will look for the Raja of Borneo for you and deliver your message."

"Tell the Raja of Borneo that the Raja of All Tigers demands food sent to him every month," the tiger-minister said. "If he refuses to do this, we shall attack in seven days. And this," he extended the whisker, "pulled from the face of the Raja of All Tigers, is for your king."

"Sir," Kancil said, taking the whisker, "wait here and I shall return as soon as I have his reply."

He turned and disappeared into the forest. Kancil ran swiftly, and so did his thoughts. "Tigers' food is meat," he said aloud. "If they want food, they want meat. That includes me. No, no. I will not be anyone's dinner!"

"Most certainly not!" a voice answered. Kancil looked around and spied his friend the porcupine under a tree.

"Dear friend," he said, "may I have a hair from you? You will save our land."

"Gladly," the porcupine said. He pulled a bristle from his back.

Kancil, carrying the porcupine's bristle, hurried back to the three tigers, who were now wearing out a path with their pacing.

With great respect, Kancil said, "The Raja of Borneo said that his last battle was fought too long ago. He welcomes a war and will be looking forward to it. He, too, sends his whisker. Please take it to the Raja of All Tigers." Kancil offered the porcupine's bristle. The minister took it and saw that it was longer than the mouse-deer was tall, it was thicker than the mouse-deer's leg, it was strong and resilient.

The minister was greatly surprised. Now he bowed to Kancil and said, "I shall take your message to the Raja of All Tigers." The three left the forests of Borneo and returned to Java, where the Raja of All Tigers waited impatiently.

The minister was afraid to give his message, but, scraping the floor in his very low bow, he said, "Oh, Fiercest-of-the-Most-Fierce, the Raja of Borneo desires war. He sends his whisker to you." With this, the minister passed the porcupine bristle to his king.

The Raja of All Tigers gazed at it from all angles with a very thoughtful expression on his face. At last he said, "I have decided. Borneo is too far for us. We shall demand food from the elephants of Sumatra."

NOTES

It is true that the natural habitat of tigers includes most of Asia and, in Indonesia, the islands of Java, Bali, and Sumatra, but not Borneo.

Kancil, the tiny mouse-deer, is encountered in many Indonesian folktales. In spite of his size, he is usually portrayed as being clever enough to gain the upper hand. His wit and intelligence, not his physical size, keep him alive, and Indonesian children delight in listening to stories about Kancil.

The mouse-deer is an animal native to parts of Southeast Asia. It lives in the lowland forests or bushes near rivers, but extensive exploitation of forests has caused it to become an endangered species.

The tiger, too, is in danger of extinction in Indonesia. It is believed to be almost nonexistent in Java.

Sulawesi
and
Nusa Tenggara

A Toraja Tale

MANY years ago in Toraja, there lived a clever young boy who was a servant in the raja's household. More than he wanted anything else in the world, he wanted to be noticed by the raja.

One day, he happened to see the raja prepare for a bath in a large pool of clear water that was surrounded by blossoming lilies and plants. The raja slipped off his ring and placed it carefully on a stone before he stepped into the water.

Aha! the boy thought. This is my chance to be known to the raja. He reached out stealthily from behind a plant and picked up the ring. He hid it well so that when the servants were searched, the ring could not be found. The raja offered a generous reward for the return of his favorite ring.

The servant boy appeared before the raja and, placing his palms together in front of him in a gesture of respect, he bowed to the raja and said, "Your Highness, I think I know where the ring is."

"Bring it here, and we'll see if it's mine," the raja answered.

To be sure, the boy had found the raja's ring! His Highness was so pleased that he showered the boy with gifts of expensive clothes and elegant food.

When the warm season came, more boats began to dock in the harbors of Sulawesi. The captain of one of these ships went ashore carrying a duck under each arm and a piece of black stick in his right hand. He requested an audience with the raja at Toraja.

"Your Highness," he said, "if you can tell me which duckling is male and which female, and which end of this stick is the bottom and which the top, I will give you my boat."

The raja looked first at one duckling, then at the other. They looked exactly alike. He saw no difference, and the raja was baffled. He then thought of the clever servant boy and sent for him.

"If you can tell me which duckling is male and which female, and which end of the stick is the top and which the bottom, you will succeed me as king," he said. "But if you fail, you forfeit your life."

The boy looked at the two ducks, but he, too, could find no difference. He thought guiltily of the ring and was sure he was being punished for hiding the ring and accepting rich rewards. Now he was sorry he had played that trick on the raja.

"Please," the boy said, "I need to think about this. Will you give me some time?"

The boy walked down to the harbor and sat down on the dock. He became so unhappy thinking of the ducks that he decided he would rather drown himself than be killed by the king. So he jumped into the water.

Instead of drowning, the boy became unconscious and was pulled from the water by the sailors of the very boat whose captain had posed the riddles to the raja.

As the boy slowly regained consciousness, he heard a voice say, "But how can the master tell which is male and which is female?"

"Easy!" a second voice answered. "Place the two ducks near water and the one that goes in the water first is the male. The female will follow."

There was general laughter among the men. "But what about that black stick?" another voice asked. "I can't tell which end is the top and which end the bottom. How is he going to do that?"

"That's easy, too," the second voice said. "Put the stick in water and the end that sinks lower is the bottom and the other end is the top."

By this time, the boy was fully conscious. He cautiously opened one eye and saw that the men were all gathered with their backs to him. He stole away quietly and ran back to the palace.

"Your Highness," he said, "I think I know the answer. May I take the ducks to the pond?"

He put the ducks down next to the water. Soon one of them went into the water and the other followed. Pointing to the one that went in first, the boy said, "That is the male. The other is the female."

"The boy is right," the captain said. Then he held up the length of black wood. "How about this?" he asked the raja. "Which end is the top and which the bottom?"

The raja took the stick and studied each end. They both looked the same. He handed it to the boy and said, "Well?"

The boy threw the stick into the water. One end dipped lower in the water than the other. Holding the lower end, he said, "This end is the bottom and the other is the top."

"Right again," the captain said.

Thus, the boy got his wish and the king gained a successor.

NOTES

Folktales often try to explain the environment. This story is an entertaining tale referring to a riddle concerning natural phenomena of the region. It comes from the Toraja people, who live in the central highlands of Sulawesi, or Celebes, the island whose shape is often compared to a crab, an orchid, or a headless octopus.

Toar and Limimuut

ONCE, a very long time ago, there was a most unusual rock in the middle of the ocean. Its top rose above the surface of the water, where the sun's rays warmed it. The heat of the sun made the rock perspire, and from this perspiration, Limimuut was born. No one was there to record how this pretty girl grew up by herself, but she did grow to become an adult on that rock.

One day, when she was grown, she stood on the rock and looked at the ocean in its restless motion. As she marveled at the vastness of the waters around her, she saw a crow circling overhead. Its beak held a branch with a few dried leaves on it. Limimuut wondered where the bird had found the stick.

The crow dipped down to her and said, "It comes from Taoere."

Limimuut was surprised and pleased that the bird could read her thoughts and speak her language.

"Will you please take me there?" she asked.

The bird agreed, so the two of them flew to Taoere. Limimuut found that she could fly like the crow.

They came to a small piece of land just emerging from the ocean. It was one of many small islands in the waters around it. The crow alighted on the little island.

"This is where I found the branch. It is called Taoere." With that, the crow flew away, leaving Limimuut alone.

She then scooped up a small handful of soil and flew home to her own rock, where she scattered the soil. As she watched, this small handful grew into a big land mass, and kept growing for nine days.

Limimuut looked around at the new land and saw that it was barren. She flew to Taoere again and brought home another handful of soil to scatter. Then something wonderful happened! Some green shoots began to push up out of the ground. This became the vegetation that gradually covered the earth.

Limimuut made a mountain on one part of this land. When the mountain was high enough, she climbed to the top and faced west. As she looked into the afternoon sky, she felt a child grow within her. Soon a healthy boy was born. She named him Toar.

Toar grew into a handsome young man who was ready to take a wife. Where can he find a wife? his mother wondered.

"Roam the world, my son," she said. And so Toar set out for other parts of the ocean to seek a woman to marry. He returned alone after traveling far.

"I found no one fit to be my wife," he said.

His mother then said, "Let's cut a piece of cane as long as I am, one for you and one for me. Then you go to your right. I shall go to my left. If you should meet a woman carrying a piece of cane longer than yours, marry her."

So Toar set out again, heading right with his cane, while his mother went left with hers. Much later, Toar met a woman coming from the opposite direction. She was carrying a cane. He put his cane against hers to measure it, and her cane was longer.

Remembering only that the woman's stick must be longer than his, he married this woman and took her home. He did not suspect that she was his mother, whose cane had grown longer than his during their travels.

They returned to Limimuut's mountain and lived there very happily. Limimuut had children three times, each time bearing nine in number.

From this family of Toar and Limimuut, the people of Minahasa came to be.

NOTES

Folk stories of different cultures often relate tales of pregnancies caused by magic. The story of Limimuut includes not only a magic pregnancy, but also the magic growth of land and vegetation, possibly with foreign origin, such as plants and soil brought back from Limimuut's travels.

This tale is from Minahasa on the northern tip of Sulawesi.

How Rice Came to Earth (2)

I N a small village long ago, a man, his wife, and two young sons lived a very comfortable life. The family owned many pigs, buffaloes, and chickens as well as fields of vegetables, making them one of the wealthiest families in their village.

One day, both parents died in an accident, leaving two orphaned boys who were too young to work on the farm and care for the animals. The boys decided to sell the animals and live on that income, but within a few days of their parents' death, evil men came at night and drove off their animals. They also entered the storage area and stole all the food.

Reduced to begging for their food in the neighborhood, the two brothers somehow managed to catch some fish in the pond their father had built. Since this was their only source of food, they guarded their fish pond day and night lest the thieves return.

Much of the burden of the work fell on the younger brother because the older boy was handicapped. He had been born with webbed feet, a condition in which his toes were attached to each other. His feet occasionally hurt so much it was painful for him to walk. On one such day, he begged his brother to allow him to rest at home.

The younger boy walked alone to the fish pond to guard it against thieves. Imagine his surprise when he found seven beautiful young women bathing in his fish pond! The boy was awed by their beauty. Each was as beautiful as a goddess.

As they prepared to leave, the boy said, "Do you mind if I join you on your journey?"

"We don't mind," they replied. "Follow us if you wish." They walked until they reached a rainbow, which turned out to be a stairway. They walked up the steps for seven days and seven nights until they reached heaven, which was home for the young women. As soon as they arrived, the seven women vanished. The boy stood there alone, not knowing what to do next. But the long walk had tired him, so he lay down to rest and fell asleep.

When he awoke, much refreshed, the boy looked around him and saw a village in the distance. He decided to walk to the village. As he approached its outskirts, he saw a man busily spreading something yellow out in the sun. The sun's rays glinted off the yellow, giving it a lovely shine.

"This must be gold," the boy thought. "I have found a treasure!"

As he came nearer, the man eyed him with suspicion. "Where did all this gold come from?" the boy asked the man.

The man laughed. "You don't really think this is gold, do you?"

"It looks like it," the boy said, "but if it's not, what is it?"

"It's rice," the farmer answered, for the man was a rice farmer. "It's for eating. Rice tastes delicious and is nourishing."

The boy looked closely at the rice and said, "I've never seen this before. Does it grow on earth?"

"No," the man said, "it only grows here in heaven. It is the most valuable and nourishing food created by the gods. Its taste is unequaled."

"If what you say is true," the boy answered, "please let me have a few grains so I can take them home with me to plant."

This made the man extremely upset. He shouted, "No! Never will I allow you to take this home!"

Seeing the surprise on the boy's face, the man softened his voice and said, "You may eat the rice here, and as much as you wish. But I forbid you to take any of it to earth."

He then gave the boy a handful of rice.

The boy ate it and found that the man did speak the truth. Rice was delicious! It also gave him renewed energy, and he no longer felt tired. Now, more than ever, the boy wanted to take the grains back to earth and plant them there. He decided to hide some in his mouth and run away to earth as soon as he had a chance.

The next day, a flock of birds settled on the paddy fields and started to eat the grain. Shouting and waving his arms, the farmer ran after the birds to chase them away. The boy grabbed a handful of grain drying in the sun, stuffed it into his mouth, and ran to the rainbow in the opening in heaven.

The farmer, returning to his farm, saw the boy's hand print in the tray of rice grain. He looked up to see the boy running to the rainbow, and he gave chase. Just as the boy reached the rainbow stairway, the farmer reached out and grabbed him by the shirt.

"Oh, no, you don't," he said, shaking the boy. He shook him so roughly that the boy's feet flew out from under him. One of his feet struck the sharp edge of the rainbow and received a deep cut on the heel. In spite of the boy's shriek of pain, the farmer ignored the wound to search the boy from head to toe. He found the rice grain in his mouth and ordered him to spit it all out.

"I warn you," he said. "Don't try this again, because the next time I catch you doing this, I'll push you through that hole where the rainbow is."

The boy just nodded miserably because his heel was throbbing with pain.

"I'm sorry," he said. "I won't try it again. But my heel is hurting so much. May I go back with you? I'll even be your slave if you let me stay. I can't go home until this heals."

The farmer felt sorry for the boy. "You can come with me," he said, "but, remember, don't try to steal my grain."

Slowly and painfully the boy limped behind the farmer back to the farm.

The rest of the day was spent caring for his injury, but the next day, the farmer set him to work chasing away the birds that came to eat the drying rice grain.

As his foot healed, his spirits began to rise, and, again, the boy began to plot his escape to earth with the rice grain. He felt that the farmer was greedy for not wanting to share his rice grain with people on earth. The wound on his heel was beginning to close, he noticed, and he would be able to leave very soon. Just then, an idea came to him.

I can push several grains of rice into this wound, he thought. He'll never think of looking there. I'll even ask his permission to go home.

So the boy stuffed a few grains of rice into his healing wound and sought the farmer.

"I would like your permission to go home, sir," he said. "My brother needs my help. Will you let me go home?"

The farmer was suspicious at first. "You have my permission," he said, "but you must allow me to inspect you very closely. I will not allow a single grain to be carried to earth."

"Yes, I understand that, sir," the boy answered. "The last time was frightening, so I will not try to rob you again."

The farmer examined the boy thoroughly but did not think of opening the healing wound. After satisfying himself that the boy carried not one grain of rice, he allowed the boy to leave heaven. As soon as the boy reached earth, he hurried to his home and planted the rice grain. He watered it, chased away the birds and insects, and weeded out other plants around it. The rice plants grew and thrived and finally, one day, the tiny grain appeared.

As the rice plants bore grain in abundance, the rice in heaven started to dry up. Rice, it seems, could grow well in heaven or earth, but not in both places at the same time. The farmer, knowing this, had tried to prevent rice grain from escaping to earth.

The farmer looked at his dying crop and thought of the boy who had gone home to earth. He concluded that, somehow, in some way, the boy had managed to steal some grain and had taken it back to earth.

The farmer called a sparrow and said, "Go to earth and see if there is some rice growing there. Be sure to come back and report to me."

The sparrow flew down to earth and saw a field of rice ripe for harvesting. He flew down into the rice plants and began feasting. After he had his fill, he flew back to heaven and reported to the farmer. If I say rice is growing on earth, he thought, then all the birds will go there to feed. But if I say there is none, then I shall have the rice to myself.

So thinking, he told the farmer, "There is no rice on earth." He did not realize that his beak had kept some evidence of his feast.

"You lie," the farmer said. "I can see bits of rice on your beak."

"If you don't believe me," the sparrow said, "send another bird."

"I will," the farmer replied. "If the dove sees that there is rice on earth, then he will kill you. If there is no rice, and you are right, then you will kill the dove."

The two birds flew down to earth, and the dove immediately saw the rice plants. He accused the sparrow of being a liar, and they fought fiercely. The sparrow lost.

As for the farmer in heaven, he no longer controlled the growth of rice, because it grew very well, and abundantly, on earth.

NOTES

This is another story explaining the origin of rice, the staple food of the people of Sulawesi. See "How Rice Came to Earth (1)" for a Javanese version.

The two versions show rice as coming to the people on earth through divine means. This points to the important place that rice cultivation holds in the culture of the rice-growing people of Sulawesi as well as of Java.

For information on the number seven, see *Kris* under More Notes on Indonesian Culture.

Ringkitan and the Cuscus

Along time ago, in a village on the beach at Minahasa, a fisherman and his wife lived with their nine beautiful daughters. The youngest of these was Ringkitan.

All nine girls were exceedingly beautiful. Their beauty was well known in their own village and in other faraway villages. Young men came from all over with proposals of marriage, but not one of these suitors would the young women accept. The men were not good enough!

Their parents never pressed the girls to accept one or another of these young men. They left that decision to their daughters. But with nine eligible young women at home and not one married, the parents felt embarrassed. They also worried about the time when no man would desire their daughters in marriage because the girls would be too old. Even now, the number of proposals had begun to dwindle.

In the midst of these concerns, the parents received a visit from a cuscus, an animal related to the possum. He wanted to marry one of their daughters. As usual, they did not pressure any of their daughters to marry but left the decision in each one's hands.

The oldest daughter was asked first.

"What!" she said. "A cuscus? That disgusting animal! Tell him to go home. I'd rather die than be his wife."

So her mother asked the second oldest daughter if she would like to marry the cuscus.

"Who wants to marry a cuscus!" she exclaimed. "Ugh! That dirty animal. Send him away!"

So her mother asked the third daughter, then the fourth, fifth, sixth, seventh, and eighth. All of them refused, saying just what their two oldest sisters had said. But when she asked her youngest and most beautiful daughter, Ringkitan replied, "He may be a cuscus, but he is kind and loving. If you approve, I don't mind marrying him."

"My dear daughter," her mother said. "I cannot make that decision for you. But if you like him and want to accept his proposal, then your father and I are very happy for you."

Ringkitan and the cuscus were married. They were very happy together, but Ringkitan was always teased by her sisters and the villagers for marrying a cuscus. Ringkitan did not mind because she loved her husband.

No one knew what the cuscus did for a living or how he supported his wife. Ringkitan only knew that he left in the morning and returned in the afternoon. Nobody knew where he went in the daytime. Her sisters teased her mercilessly, laughing at her because she, as his wife, did not know what he did or where he went. Because her sisters badgered her so much, Ringkitan decided to find out what he did.

One morning, soon after her husband had left for work, Ringkitan followed him. He walked into the forest toward some small trees and bushes. He stood still and looked around to make sure that no one had followed him. Then he took off his skin and hid it under the brushwood.

When Ringkitan saw her husband without the cuscus disguise, she wanted to jump for joy, because her husband was a man, and a very handsome young man at that. She kept quiet with difficulty while he strode quickly down to the beach, where a boat with several men waited for him.

When they were gone, Ringkitan went home, happy but puzzled. Why did he wear a disguise, she wondered.

She followed him for several days to make sure he was a real human being. Once she was sure, she thought of a way to make him shed his disguise.

As usual, one morning she followed her husband to the brushwood and saw him leave in his boat. Ringkitan then crept slowly to the brushwood where he had left his cuscus skin. The closer she crept to the brushwood, the more nervous she became. She looked around her fearfully to make sure no one was around.

The cuscus skin was on the ground wedged between the roots of the brushwood. Hesitantly she reached out for the skin.

Oh, how she wanted her sisters and the other villagers to know that her husband was not a disgusting cuscus but a really handsome young man. Her sisters always laughed at him, and the villagers chased him away when he tried to join their company. She did love her husband!

So, with trembling hands, she took her husband's cuscus skin and hid it. Then she sat under the brushwood to wait for his return.

When he returned that afternoon, she rose to greet him with a smile. Shocked, her husband turned to hide from her. Ringkitan caught his hand and said, "Don't run from me, my dear husband."

"Why did you do this?" he asked.

"I don't mean to hurt you," she said, "and I am sorry if I do. But I don't want you to hide your handsome face in the cuscus fur again."

"Why do you want me to show my real face?" he asked.

"Every day my sisters and the people in the village laugh at me for being married to a cuscus," she said.

"And you?" he asked. "Are you ashamed to have a cuscus for a husband?"

"No," she said emphatically. "I was never ashamed of having a cuscus for a husband. That's why I chose to marry you in the first place."

"Then why do you want me to appear as I really am?" he asked. "Why now?"

"People, and especially my sisters, always tease me for having a cuscus for a husband," she said. "Now that I know you are really a handsome man, I want them to know that you are not a disgusting cuscus. They will be sorry they laughed at me. Please, if you love me, stay the way you are."

"Very well," he said, "if that is what you want."

Hand in hand, they walked home together. "Everybody has a name," Ringkitan said. "What is yours?"

"My name is Kusoi," he said.

"Kusoi! Kusoi!" she repeated. "What a beautiful name! After all this time, only now do I know my husband's name." They smiled at each other.

After this, Ringkitan and Kusoi seemed to be happier than ever. Not so her sisters. When they found out that Kusoi was a handsome man and not a cuscus, they became jealous of Ringkitan. They wanted Kusoi for themselves. They wracked their brains to think of a way to take Kusoi away from Ringkitan.

Then, one day, Kusoi said, "My dearest wife, I have dreamed of making a fortune in a distant land. I have planned for a long time to go, and I have just heard that the time is ripe. Would you mind very much if I left for many days? It may be several moons."

"I do not want you to go," Ringkitan said, "but I can see you are determined. I shall miss you terribly. Every day that you are gone, I shall pray that you come home safely, successful in whatever you plan to do."

Soon after, Kusoi sailed away. Ringkitan was very sad to see him go, but her sisters were happy. This was the chance they had been waiting for. Now they planned and plotted in earnest so they could have Kusoi. They finally agreed that as long as Ringkitan was alive, Kusoi would never have eyes for anyone else. The only thing to do was to kill her.

When news came to the village that Kusoi was finally coming home, Ringkitan was ecstatic. Her husband was coming home at last! She could hardly wait to go to the seashore to greet him.

Her sisters were also happy that Kusoi was coming home. They insisted on accompanying Ringkitan to the seashore, showing her how much they shared in her happiness. Ringkitan, of course, had no idea what her sisters intended to do.

They reached the seashore, and the nine sisters played and laughed together happily. Many tall shade trees with strong and sturdy branches grew on the fringes of this shore. Children liked to swing from the branches, and so did the sisters.

Beginning with the eldest, all the sisters had a chance to be pushed in the swing. When Ringkitan's turn came, the eight sisters together pushed her higher and higher. The sisters kept laughing and chattering so that Ringkitan was not aware of their intention. Then they pushed her so hard that she swung to the tree's topmost branch, where her hair became entangled. Suspended over the water, Ringkitan called for help, but no one except her sisters heard her.

They turned a deaf ear to her pleas for help. They were positive that Ringkitan would die in the tree without anyone else knowing. They hurried home before someone discovered their misdeed.

Ringkitan continued to struggle to free herself from the branches, but her hair was thick and wavy and hopelessly entangled in the branches. She realized then that her sisters had done this with evil intent.

Ringkitan looked at the ocean and saw a line of sailing ships come over the horizon. They were headed in her direction.

The first ship passed under her tree. She sang,

> *Captain of the wooden boat*
> *sturdily afloat,*
> *have mercy upon me,*
> *unhappy, miserable me.*
> *Tell me, please,*
> *where my husband Kusoi be.*

A voice from below carried up to her, "Kusoi is coming."
Then a second boat hove into sight. Ringkitan sang,

> *Captain of the wooden boat*
> *carved in patterns ornate,*
> *have mercy upon me,*
> *unhappy, miserable me.*
> *Tell me, please,*
> *where my husband Kusoi be.*

A voice from below answered her, "Kusoi's coming. He is still in the rear."

Then Ringkitan saw a third boat, this one made of copper. She sang,

> *Captain of the copper boat,*
> *vessel of light,*
> *have mercy upon me,*
> *unhappy, miserable me.*
> *Tell me, please,*
> *where my husband Kusoi be.*

A voice from below answered, "Kusoi is coming. He's still in the rear." Ringkitan strained to see the next ship. It was made of tin. Again, she sang her lament, asking for Kusoi. Again, a voice answered her. The next boat was made of bronze, the one after that of silver. Each time the answer was the same, "He is coming." A splendid boat made of gold followed the silver boat. Ringkitan sang,

> Owner of the gold boat,
> bright as the sun,
> have mercy upon me,
> unhappy, miserable me.
> Tell me, please,
> where my husband Kusoi be.

The ship stopped under her. A richly dressed young man stood on the deck and looked up at Ringkitan.

"Who are you?" he asked.

"I am Ringkitan," she answered.

The young man looked at her closely. Satisfied, he said, "I am Kusoi, your husband. How did you get yourself into that position?"

"My sisters swung me," Ringkitan explained. "When I became trapped up here, they left me. Please help me untangle my hair so I can come down to you."

Kusoi climbed the tree quickly and loosened her hair from the branches. He helped her down to the ship, then demanded, "Tell me exactly what happened."

Ringkitan told him about coming to the beach, taking turns swinging, and how her sisters ignored her cries and left.

Kusoi listened silently. Then, shaking his head, he said, "Your sisters are evil. Don't worry. I am back for good, and I shall take care of this. Now, climb into this trunk. We will not let your sisters know that you are with me."

The news of Kusoi's arrival traveled quickly through the village. Everyone came down to see the fortune that each man had brought home. They marveled at the men, especially at Kusoi. His fortune was the greatest. Dressed like a prince, he also carried himself like one. All of Ringkitan's sisters dressed in their best and waited for him. Each had prepared a special dish for Kusoi and served him, hoping to gain his attention all to herself. But all Kusoi asked of them was, "Where is Ringkitan? Why isn't she here to greet me?"

Her sisters replied, "We saw her go to the seashore to wait for you. Wasn't she there when you landed?"

Kusoi invited the people to his home and entertained them with stories of his adventures on the high seas and in other countries.

"As I was landing here on the beach," he said, "I saw a woman in pain, stuck on the top of the tree and entangled in its branches. So I went to help her."

Each of the eight sisters turned pale. "Where is she now?" they asked.

"Let me finish my story," Kusoi said. "My servants will bring her here later." And Kusoi continued with his adventures while the eight sisters fidgeted in anxiety.

Soon the maid escorted a beautiful young woman, wearing a gorgeous dress with jewelry, to the seat next to Kusoi. The young woman's beauty was breathtaking. She and Kusoi made a handsome couple. Unable to take their eyes off the woman, the guests realized that she was none other than Ringkitan.

"This is the woman I rescued from the tree today," Kusoi said. "Do you know that this is my wife Ringkitan? Somebody tried to kill her. I don't have to tell you who was responsible, because the people who are know what they did. I do not plan to punish them."

Before the night was over, Ringkitan's sisters came to her one by one and asked forgiveness and promised not to do anything so mean again. They never again bothered Ringkitan and Kusoi, who, from then on, lived in great wealth and great happiness.

NOTES

This story comes from Minahasa. It shows how true loyalty can be rewarding.

The cuscus is a slow-moving marsupial found in the rain forests of Sulawesi, New Guinea, northern Australia, and nearby islands. It has a thick coat of fur, large round protruding eyes with vertical pupils, long claws, and a prehensile tail that can grasp things by wrapping itself around them. The male of the spotted cuscus species is yellow or white with dark spots.

La Dana and His Buffalo

L<small>A</small> Dana was the son of a farmer from Toraja. Although his father was neither rich nor very poor, La Dana had a most fertile mind with a richness of ideas.

La Dana and his friend were invited to a funeral feast. As was the custom in Toraja, everyone had a share of the buffalo meat. Since each person's standing within the community decided how much and which part of the animal would be his or her share, La Dana received half of each of the buffalo's hind legs. His friend, however, received a whole buffalo except for the two half hind legs.

"I have an idea," La Dana said. "Why don't we put your share and mine together? Then we'll have a whole buffalo, and maybe a live one!"

"And we can raise it!" his friend said. "That's a great idea! Let's find out if we can have a live one."

Their host agreed to give them a live animal. Very happy, the two boys went home with their buffalo.

A few days later, La Dana said, "I'm hungry for buffalo. Let's kill the animal and eat it."

"No, I want to wait until the buffalo grows," his friend replied.

"That's all right," La Dana answered. "I will just take my share. I shall cut half of the hind legs off, and you can raise the animal yourself."

"But if you cut its legs," his friend protested, "the buffalo may die. Tell you what—I'll give you part of my share, the other half of the back legs, so you'll have two whole back legs. But promise not to kill it."

"Oh, all right," La Dana answered. He went home, very happy.

Several days went by. Then, in the light of the full moon, La Dana walked over to his friend's home and said, "My best friend, let's kill the buffalo now because I'm having a party tomorrow night and I need the meat."

His friend was surprised and distressed. "Wait a while longer until it's bigger," he said. "If you'll wait and promise not to kill it, I'll give you some of my share—the two front legs."

"All right, if you say so," La Dana replied and went home, very happy.

It was the time of the full moon again when La Dana went to see his friend.

"The buffalo's grown big," he told his friend. "Let's kill the animal now. I haven't eaten meat for a long time."

"Be patient," his friend replied. "It's not time to kill it yet."

"Well," La Dana said, hesitating, "I'll cut my share, and you can raise the buffalo yourself."

"If you'll wait a little longer," his friend said, "I'll give you all my share except the head." La Dana went home, very happy.

But a few days later, he was back at his friend's house. His friend was in the middle of some work when La Dana approached him. "Let's kill the buffalo," he told his friend. "I want to eat it."

His friend lost his temper and said, "Why don't you take that whole buffalo for yourself and not bother me any more!"

La Dana did just that, very, very happily. He took the buffalo home and raised it until it was huge!

NOTES

This is another tale from Tana Toraja, the land of Toraja.

In the traditional Toraja community, the people observe a funeral ritual sometimes known as the Feast of the Dead.

This is a major cultural event in the life of the village. The corpse is left in a partially embalmed state in the back of the house or in a temporary grave, while elaborate preparations are made for its final burial. These funeral preparations can take weeks or

months, but to gather financial resources to pay for such an event often takes longer. For one thing, heads of freshly slaughtered pigs and buffalo are used.

The animal is prepared according to a certain procedure. Its blood is drained from its throat, then its feet and tail are cut. The people then wait for the animal to die, if it is not dead by then, before they butcher it. The meat is divided and distributed among the guests according to each person's rank and status in the community. The story "La Dana and His Buffalo" is based on this tradition.

The Overflowing Pot

On the tiny island of Roti, there once lived a widow with her granddaughter. They lived in a *kampung,* or village, one of many that dotted the island. Although their home was a one-room house sitting on a small lot, there was enough space in the backyard to raise vegetables. They grew beans, peanuts, sweet potatoes, and cassava.

They did not grow enough for the old woman and child to sustain themselves, so, early each morning, Grandmother went to the ocean to fish. While she was gone, the child cooked the rice and waited for Grandmother to return. Then, together, they cleaned and grilled the fish for their meals.

One morning, before she left, Grandmother said, "When you cook the rice today, use only one grain of rice. That will be enough for the two of us."

The grandchild was surprised to hear this but said nothing. When she was ready to cook, she stood indecisively by the rice pot. "How can one grain be enough for us?" she asked herself. "It is difficult to cook just one grain. Grandmother must have made a mistake. I shall cook as always." She measured the usual two handfuls of rice.

After a while, she lifted the pot cover to peep in. The rice was like a porridge and puffed to the top of the pot. The girl could not replace the cover because the rice kept pushing it up. Then the rice porridge started to flow down the sides of the pot. The girl tried to stop it, first with her broom, then with her mop. She ran back and forth in that little house, trying to sweep the porridge back to the pot. When that didn't work, she tried mopping the porridge off the floor. But the rice kept flowing out of the pot, filling the one-room house.

"Oh, stop! Stop!" the girl cried with tears flowing as freely as the rice porridge. She opened the door and ran to look for Grandmother. The rice porridge crept out the door and down the path behind the girl.

Just then, she saw Grandmother walking up the path from the sea with fish for their meal.

"Grandmother!" the girl cried. "I cooked the usual two handfuls of rice, and it overflowed from the pot, filled the house, and followed me here. Look!" And she pointed to the rice creeping along the path behind her.

"Didn't I tell you to cook just one grain of rice?" Grandmother demanded, furious at being disobeyed. In her anger, she snatched a stick from the ground and beat her granddaughter. "Disobedient girl!" she cried.

The girl screamed in pain and fell down.

Then, to her surprise, Grandmother saw the girl disappear before her very eyes. She blinked, and there was a monkey in place of the girl. Hopping on one foot, then the other, the monkey laughed and jumped onto the branch of a tree and said, "Grandmother, you won't have me to help you any more. You will not have anyone to talk to or to take care of you." The monkey disappeared.

The old woman was alone. She truly had no one to talk to or to cook her rice for her. Why, oh why, she wondered, did she have to beat her grandchild?

NOTES

Roti is one of the southernmost islands in Indonesia and is part of the group of islands called Nusa Tenggara. The weather on Roti resembles that of Australia and is drier than the area west of Bali. Most of the people on this island are said to be Christians, but many still practice animism, a belief that objects, such as animals, plants, and stones, have hidden powers.

It is said that the boys and girls of Roti are never beaten, because the people are afraid the children may turn into monkeys and leave their parents to look after themselves in their old age.

Irian Jaya

The Sago Palm

IRIPU and Tipa, two brothers from the village of Nariki, decided to leave home at the foot of the Charles Louis Mountains to visit other villages. Miripu went east and Tipa went west.

After walking for several days, Miripu came to the Mutapya River. The cool water looked so inviting he decided to rest his tired feet. Stretching out on a low-lying branch, he dropped his feet into the cool water. It was so pleasant that Miripu fell asleep, unaware that his long curly hair had also dropped into the water. The black curly hair bobbing in the water attracted a parako fish, who called the mona fish to come with it to investigate. They began to chew Miripu's hair, eating it bite by bite.

Miripu got up suddenly and sat up. His long curly hair was gone! He felt his head and discovered that his hair was short. Upset, he quickly drew his bow and arrow and shot the parako fish. The arrow hit the fish near the edge of its body, going through both sides.

In great pain, the parako fish rolled over and over, trying to work the arrow out of its body. When it finally succeeded, it was left with two black spots, one on each side.

While Miripu watched the fish, he heard the voices of women in conversation. Surprised, he looked in the direction from which the voices came. He saw two women carrying firewood. He looked around for an excuse to attract their attention. Seeing a *jatiri* fruit, he picked it and bit into it before throwing it at the women.

The fruit rolled by one woman and hit the other. She picked it up and saw Miripu's teeth marks.

"Look," she told her companion, indicating the marks, "there is someone nearby."

They looked around and saw Miripu step out from the trees near the river.

"I am Miripu from the Amota-we family of Nariki," he said. "Where are you from?"

"We are from the village of Kipya, near the ocean," they said. Miripu was pleased to hear this because he had hoped to visit a coastal village.

The two women built a fire and roasted their staple food, gum. Taken from a tree, the gum had been dried and hardened in the sun. Miripu looked at the gum and asked, "Is this all you have to eat?"

He reached into his bag and took out a few pieces of sago. Giving each woman a piece, he said, "Taste it." Then he popped a piece into his mouth to chew. The women copied him and began to chew their pieces. They smiled broadly and murmured, "Delicious. M-m-m. What is this?"

"This is sago," Miripu said. "We eat it as our daily food. We can make it and keep it for a while."

"Why don't you come with us to Tamu Upya, the region where we come from?" they asked. "We must tell everyone that sago is better than gum."

When they reached Tamu Upya, Miripu was warmly received by the villagers, especially after the women told them about his staple food, sago.

Miripu had enough sago to let the people sample it. They were enthusiastic.

"This is better than gum!" they said.

"Tell us how to make this. It's delicious!"

"Let us go and get some sago right away."

Miripu led a group to the sago forest, which was near land owned by Omaoma and her sister Pasay, leaders of the village and relatives of Miripu. The two sisters permitted the people from Kipya to build a temporary hut, where they lived while Miripu taught them how to prepare his people's staple food, sago.

First, Miripu cut an old stem of sago palm, with the top portion going to the young women, the middle portion to the middle-aged women, and the largest part, the bottom, to the old women. The stem was then beaten and pressed and its starch extracted and collected and dried in the sun.

The sun-dried sago was thick and hard, but it was chewy and filling. The supply of sago slowly filled the basket and the storage sack. At last the Kipya people had learned to prepare sago and had provided themselves with enough to take home. With Miripu accompanying them, they traveled back to Kipya, where they immediately built a communal dining hut.

The people of Kipya appreciated the great favor Miripu had done for them. In return, they introduced him to a young Kipya maiden. Just as they had hoped, Miripu fell in love with the pretty young woman. He married her and took her home to Nariki.

A year later, a son was born to Miripu and his wife. The little child was stubborn, with a will to do as he pleased without regard to his parents' wishes. As he grew older, this trait did not go away.

One day, Miripu's wife said, "I would like to visit my family. They have not met our son yet, and he is almost a young man."

So, with his brother Tipa, his wife, and his son, Miripu traveled to Kipya to visit their relatives.

The people were very happy to see Miripu again. The relatives were delighted with Miripu's son and kept him busy during his visit.

One day, Miripu's son went to the seashore with a group of women to collect grubs, a type of woodworm. While the women were busy looking for the woodworm, Miripu's son went off alone with one of the young women without obtaining her mother's permission. Because he was considered to be an outsider and a guest, such behavior was not acceptable and was regarded as an insult to his hosts.

"I am deeply embarrassed by my son's behavior," Miripu told the chief of the tribe. "I humbly apologize. It is my fault for not having better control over him."

"You have done us such great service," the chief said. "This makes it very difficult for me to take action, but the people want me to do something about this insult. Your son's behavior has brought us shame."

Nothing Miripu said made any difference.

After much soul-searching, the chief decided that the Kipya people should return to their original home near Ajundua across the Irua River.

Everybody, including all the Amota-we people, felt terrible about this. Omaoma, as head of the landholders and a relative of the offender, felt some responsibility. Being a woman, she could also sympathize with those women who had felt insulted by the incident. As a result, she decided to leave her home. She entered the jungle and was never seen again.

Before she left, Omaoma gathered her family and said, "Remember, when you cut the sago palms, leave two or three standing. Do not cut all of them before you move on. In this way, you will always have food."

The people followed Omaoma's advice, and they have never starved.

NOTES

Miripu's son broke an unwritten law that dictated the behavior of every person in the village he was visiting. This was a grave offense in this community.

Sago palms grow abundantly on the south coast of Irian Jaya and the neighboring Maluku Islands. The natives allow a sago palm tree to grow for twenty years before cutting it down. The low-protein starch is then collected from the pulp of the trunk and sun-dried, as in the story. After several days, the men go back to the fallen tree to gather and eat the protein-rich grubs now growing in the plundered trunk. Sago serves as the staple food of the people of Irian Jaya, who eat it roasted, as porridge, or as pancakes.

The Magic Crocodile

NCE in ancient Irian, Towjatuwa, a man from the village of Sawja, looked in the Tami River for a smooth stone to make a stone adze. As he looked, he thought of the coming birth of his child and the coming death of his wife. It was believed, in that distant time, that women could not give birth naturally but needed to have an operation using a stone adze to aid in the birth. The mother's death was almost sure to follow this procedure.

Sadly Towjatuwa thought of his wife, who had worked by his side in the fields and in the home. If only, he thought, she could live.

While he thought and searched, he heard an unfamiliar voice behind him. He turned around and nearly fainted from shock and fright. A huge crocodile was walking slowly toward him. It was so enormous that Towjatuwa could not estimate its length. Nor was its appearance like anything he had seen before. Between the scales on its back were feathers of the cassowary bird, giving it a frightful appearance.

"What are you doing?" the crocodile asked in a friendly voice.

Towjatuwa could not answer for a while but, somehow, he sensed that he was in no danger from the crocodile.

"My wife is due to have her baby any day now, so I am looking for a stone to make an adze," Towjatuwa answered.

"An operation is not necessary," the crocodile said. "If you will tell me where you live, I shall come tonight and help her so that your wife will not die."

Towjatuwa was overjoyed. When he told his wife, she cried with happiness.

That night, they waited in their thatched hut for the crocodile to come. The man had made an opening in his wall for the crocodile while his wife tried to make herself comfortable by the fire.

After darkness fell, they heard the rustling of tall grass, and the crocodile entered their home slowly, holding special herbs and medicines in its mouth. It covered the mother's body with herbs.

Late that night, the baby was born, naturally and safely. Towjatuwa's wife lived. The baby was a handsome boy, and his proud parents asked the crocodile to name him. He was named Narrowra. The crocodile's name was Watuwe.

"Narrowra will grow up to be an exceptionally fine hunter," Watuwe said. "But people will kill me with an arrow, then cut me up and eat my flesh. Kwembo, the All-Powerful, will be terribly upset by this act and will punish the people by sending water to flood the earth. This is what you must do. Listen and remember well. You and Narrowra must not eat my flesh. If you do, you will die with the others. When they cut my body, ask them for my scrotum and take it to Mount Sankria. The Jankwenk, Angels of the Sky, will be there. They will tell you what you must do."

The years went by and Narrowra grew into young manhood and was an exceptional hunter, just as Watuwe had predicted.

One day, the children of the village lit a fire of dried leaves and twigs on the banks of the Tami River and placed fruit next to the fire. One of the children stood by the fruit and noticed that he became wet at the same time that the fire sputtered, as if doused by water, though there was no rain.

After this happened for the third time, the children made a veil of palm leaves and hung it on a tree. One of the children hid behind this veil and watched to see if the sprinkling of water happened again.

In a few minutes, the tall grass along the banks of the Tami River swayed and parted to reveal an enormous crocodile, who crawled up to the fireplace and fruit. It stood on the fire and extinguished it.

The child who saw all of this was shaken by the sight of the

crocodile and could not speak for a while. After the crocodile disappeared into the river, the child climbed down from the tree and ran to tell the people of the village. The story of the crocodile excited the villagers, and they planned to capture it.

They built a thatched wall near the bank, and the young men waited behind it with bows and arrows. Soon the huge crocodile with cassowary feathers between his scales came out of the water to stand upon the fire. While he stood to extinguish the fire, all the men released their arrows, piercing its neck and head and killing it.

The people were jubilant. The animal was so huge with so much meat that they could invite everyone from the surrounding villages to come and celebrate with them. The women prepared porridge while the men skinned and cut up the crocodile.

Towjatuwa and Narrowra had just returned from hunting. They heard the story of the kill told with glee, but Towjatuwa remembered Watuwe's instructions and, with a heavy heart, only asked for the scrotum, passing his share of meat to others.

Towjatuwa also remembered the rest of Watuwe's instructions. He turned to Narrowra and said, "Call your friend Kunebuan and his sister Mambawa and your sister Ubara. Quickly now!" As soon as they assembled, he led them out of the village toward Mount Sankria.

On the way, they passed deserted villages whose settlers had gone to the celebration at Sawja by the Tami River. The small group reached Mount Sankria that evening and found four Jankwenk waiting for them.

The faces of the Jankwenk were beautiful and their winged bodies pure white. Each carried a large flute. They told Towjatuwa that, for killing Watuwe, all living people, animals, and plants would be destroyed. Only those at the top of Mount Sankria would be spared. Towjatuwa and his small group had the responsibility for rebuilding the earth, replacing the people, animals, and plants with the seeds the Jankwenk would give them.

After long instructions to Towjatuwa and his group, the Jankwenk, each facing a point of the compass, lifted their flutes to play them. What sounded was not music but deafening noise. It was a clamoring that signaled the waters to flood all the corners of the earth.

A great commotion on earth followed, with claps of thunder, falling trees, and floodwaters agitated by ocean waves.

All on earth drowned except for Towjatuwa and his little group on the summit of Mount Sankria. After several days, the rains ceased and the floodwaters stopped rising. Gradually, the water level began to fall. The only tree left standing was an ironwood growing from the summit of Mount Sankria.

Towjatuwa then followed the instructions left by the Jankwenk. He released a kangaroo at the foot of the hill but it returned, a sign that the ground below was still sodden. After a few days, he released a parrot, and it, too, returned. After another few days, a pig was freed at the foot of the hill, and it did not return.

Narrowra scattered the banana seeds from the Jankwenk, and immediately banana trees grew. Narrowra and his helpers cut the banana stems. Some pieces were large and some were small. Each piece was placed with others similar in size.

Then Narrowra stood in front of them and said, "Stems, become women!" Right away, the large stems became women with large bodies and the small pieces became women with small bodies. Narrowra led these women into the jungle to choose a place to build a home.

After settling the women, Narrowra scattered more banana seeds and chopped the banana trees that sprang up. Gathering the pieces according to size, he stood in front of them and said, "Stems, become men!" Small-bodied men, large-bodied men, and medium-sized men appeared.

"Men!" Narrowra addressed them. "We have survived a great disaster, so let us have a party to commemorate it. I will make a flute while you hunt for pig."

Towjatuwa went to look for the women and found them dancing. This gave him an idea how to get the men and women together. He wanted to discuss this idea with Narrowra, but his son was busy carving a flute out of a piece of wood. Narrowra took a long time to finish the flute, and the only thing he would say, when asked if he was finished, was "Me-kek"—"I haven't finished yet."

The men returned with the pig before the flute was done. When Towjatuwa discussed his plan for the men to dance with the women, they agreed.

When they reached the women's home, the men climbed the steps to the living quarters. Narrowra took the ladder away, then signaled the men to blow their flutes. The loud sounds reverberated and scared the women, who ran here and there, looking for the ladder.

The men then decorated themselves with red, black, and white colors, forming little squares on their bodies, like layers of scales. The dancers' bodies resembled the scales of Watuwe. Each dancer wore a head decoration made of rattan and cassowary feathers. The rattan frame rested on the wrists and stood about a meter above their heads. The feathers of the cassowary bird covered the supports of the frame. White cockatoo feathers decorated the top, and the whole frame was topped by a live cassowary bird.

The dance began with the shrill sound of a flute, with short and long blasts sounding repeatedly throughout the performance.

Women, drawn by curiosity, pressed forward to observe. Narrowra, who was waiting for this to happen, found suitable partners for them, the large women partnered with large men and small women with small men.

After the dances were done, Narrowra gave plant seeds to each couple. He instructed them how to plant and care for the seeds, especially sago. He directed each couple to a specific location and told them how to establish and develop a village. In this way, the villages of Kuana, Wambes, Jetti, Kwini, Cirere, Sawja, Njai, and others came to be.

After everyone was settled and they had fulfilled the instructions of the Jankwenk, Narrowra and Kunebuan also settled down, Kunebuan marrying Ubara and Narrowra marrying Mambawa. They settled on Mount Sankria and lived a happy and peaceful life, blessed by the piece of Watuwe that Narrowra had inherited from Towjatuwa. That piece was kept in a special container called the *nokking*. The *nokking* was hung under the roof of the house, out of reach and unknown to the women.

One day Narrowra went hunting and found that nothing went right. He tripped, became tangled in roots, and his arrows repeatedly missed their mark. He felt that something was wrong and hurried home.

The women, meanwhile, had discovered the *nokking*, and

one of them had climbed to bring it down. Narrowra walked into the hut just as the women were peeling the dry leaves that covered the *nokking*.

"What is this you are doing!" he bellowed, so angry was he. "Out of this house, right away!"

Narrowra rewrapped and retied the sacred heirloom. He then ordered the people of Arso to care for the *nokking*. They tied it to a branch of the ironwood tree that had survived the great flood and took it home to Arso. It was placed in a special room in a house that was restricted to men, and guarded day and night.

If the heirloom were damaged, the people believed, another huge flood would occur. For this reason, the people of Irian Jaya for generations closely guarded the heirloom that was a part of Watuwe.

NOTES

Between Sekanto and Arso, there is a place called Me-kek. It is supposed to be the spot where Narrowra carved his flute and repeatedly answered *"Me-kek"* to his father's question, "Are you finished yet?"

Tales of great floods, as in this story, are found in the mythology of most cultures.

According to Suyadi Pratomo, who originally narrated this story, the Watuwe heirloom was opened in November 1953 by some youths. It contained two large stone adzes.

More Notes on Indonesian Culture

RORO KIDUL

People in Central Java hold many beliefs about Roro Kidul.

In the sixteenth century Roro Kidul and the first ruler of the Mataram Kingdom, Panembahan Senapati, were said to have made an agreement. Panembahan Senapati was in the middle of a war and needed reinforcements. Roro Kidul promised to help him on one condition, that he and all of his descendants become her husbands. He agreed. Panembahan Senapati's descendants include all the kings from Surakarta and Jogjakarta palaces, and it is widely believed in Java that Roro Kidul still comes to the palaces to visit her husbands. She arrives in a golden carriage pulled by eight flying horses, accompanied by her followers the ghosts and a downpour of rain. People living around the palaces hear the sound of her ghosts, a peculiar sound called "*lampor*," and they immediately lock themselves in their homes.

Within each palace, a special room is set apart at a higher elevation than the other rooms and is designated for the sole purpose of the meeting between Roro Kidul and the king.

People in Central Java also believe that in the month of Syawal, which falls after the Islamic fasting month, they can go to a certain place in the South Sea, over the home of Roro Kidul. During this visit, no one is allowed to speak.

Bathers swimming or playing on the beach close to Roro Kidul's home are careful not to wear anything green, because the queen supposedly claims that color as hers and is angered to see it on anyone else. When a person in that area disappears, people believe that Roro Kidul is to blame.

Once a year on the first of the month of Suro, the kings from Jogjakarta and Surakarta palaces traditionally go to the South Sea to hold a ceremony called "Labuhan," a word derived from the ancient Javanese word "*labuh*," meaning "cause something to float away to the middle of the sea carried by waves." In the Labuhan ceremony, the kings offer specific gifts to Roro Kidul. These gifts are nail clippings and hair cuttings of the king, various foods prepared in certain prescribed ways, and women's clothes for Roro Kidul.

These gifts are placed within a large wooden-lidded box, which is placed in the water. As it floats away from the shore, the king and his followers wait on the beach for it to return. If the box comes back empty, then the gifts have been accepted by Roro Kidul.

Kris or Keris

A man's *kris,* his dagger, is believed to represent him, thus giving it an importance beyond its mere physical use as a weapon.

Outwardly, the shape of the *kris* often represents a *naga,* or snake. Its hilt may be carved in ivory with *raksasa* (demon) images to drive away the evil spirits.

The grip on a nobleman's *kris* holds gold, rubies, diamonds, and sapphires. The blade is ridged and sharp, giving it a "wavy" look. The number of *lok* (waves or ridges) is usually seven or nine but may be as high as thirty-one, always an odd number because it assures good luck. Ornaments on the blade such as leaves, garuda, or *naga* signify protection. Both handle and blade decorations use traditional designs.

The Javanese and Balinese believe that the *kris* has a soul of its own. Some are believed to have the power to talk, fly, turn into a snake, or even father human children. If the blade is pointed at someone or inserted into the shadow or footprint of an intended victim, it is capable of killing that person.

The proper way for a man to wear a *kris* is at his back, fastened in the girdle, positioned so that the lower end of the sheath is on his left and the grip is above the girdle on his right.

Women of the palace also wear a *kris* in the same position, but theirs are worn in front. A woman's *kris* is smaller.

Clothing

The traditional attire for Javanese women consists of the *kain* and *kebaya.* The *kain* is usually made of a batik fabric and serves as a skirt. It is wrapped around the waist and lower body and covers the body from waist to ankle. The *kebaya* is the blouse worn with the *kain.* Lovely, sheer fabrics are used for special occasions.

The *sarong* is a wrap-around skirt much like the *kain.* This is worn by men when they go to the mosque and on informal occasions.

The girdle is a wide band that encircles the waist over the *kain.* Men wear a girdle and *kain* to a wedding if they happen to be the groom, father of the bride, or father of the groom. The groom, in addition, wears a *kris* under the girdle.

CLIMATE

The climate in Indonesia is always hot and humid, with the temperature remaining about the same throughout the year. Cooler temperatures occur as the elevation increases, but only the tallest mountains in Irian Jaya have snow.

Because the Indonesian archipelago is within the equatorial zone, rainfall is almost a daily occurrence with wide variation from place to place. Most parts of Sumatra, Kalimantan, Sulawesi, and Irian Jaya have a great deal of tropical rainfall all year while Java and the other islands have monsoon seasons.

During the West Monsoon, the wind blows down from the South China Sea and the islands have drenching rainfall with high humidity from November through April. Afternoon thundershowers occur frequently.

The East Monsoon blows hot, dry air from Australia between May and October. This wind affects especially the islands east of Java from Bali to Timor and Roti. The closer the islands are to Australia, the longer the dry season. Kalimantan and Sumatra, both far from Australia, have no dry season.

Sources

Alibasah, Margaret M., retold by. *Indonesian Folk Tales.* Djakarta: Penerbit Djambatan, 1975.

  "The Crocodile and the Monkey" ("Buaya and Beruk")
  "Pak Dungu" ("Pa Dungu")
  "The Buffalo Wins!" ("The Story of Minangkabau")
  "Ringkitan and the Cuscus"

Aman, S. D. B. *Folk Tales from Indonesia.* Djakarta: Penerbit Djambatan, 1976.

  "Toar and Limimuut"
  "The Story of Sangkuriang"
  "The Overflowing Pot"

Boyer, Gabriel Mario. *Land Dayak Folk Tales.* Illustrated by Krisno Jitab. Borneo Literature Bureau, 1971.

  "Why We Have Insects, Bees, and Birds" ("The Coming of Insects and Birds")
  "No Tigers in Borneo"

Dakeyne, Marian. *Cerita Rakyat Dan Dongeng Dari Indonesia* (Folktales and Legends from Indonesia). Illustrated by Marianne Collins. Melbourne: Edward Arnold (Australia) PTY Ltd., 1976.

  "The Buffalo Wins!" ("Asal Usul Nama 'Minangkabau'")
  "The Crying Stone" ("Batu Menangis")
  "The Green Princess" ("Puteri Hijau")
  "The Origin of Thunder, Lightning, Rainbow, and Rain" ("Asal Usul Adanya Pelangi, Kilat, Guntur, dan Hujan")
  "The Story of Sangkuriang"
  "The Palace at Solo" ("Asal Usul Kraton Surakarta [Solo]")
  "The Legendary Jaka Tarub" ("Joko Tarub")
  "The Mosque" ("Asal Usul Mesjid Demak")
  "Out of Harm's Way" ("Timun Mas")
  "Creation of the Bali Channel" ("Asal Usul Selat Bali")
  "The Tragedy of Jayaprana"
  "La Dana and His Buffalo" ("La Dana dan Kerbaunya")
  "No Tigers in Borneo" ("Mengapa Tidak Ada Harimau di Kalimantan")

deLeeuw, Adele. *Indonesian Legends and Folk Tales.* Illustrated by Ronni Solbert. New York: Thomas Nelson and Sons, 1964.

  "Kerta's Sin" ("Segara Anakan")

Knappert, Jan. *Myths and Legends of Indonesia.* Singapore: Heinemann Educational Books (Asia) Ltd., 1977.
    "One Sun" ("Why There Is Only One Sun")
    "Kerta's Sin" ("The Son Who Sinned")
    "Tiung Wanara" ("The Founding of the Kingdom of Majapahit")
    "The Woman and the Fishes"
    "The Story of Sangkuriang" ("The Legend of the Boat Mountain")
    Creation myth in the Preface
Koutsouokis, Albert, translator. *Indonesian Folk Tales.* Illustrated by Jean Elder. Adelaide: Rigby Ltd., 1970.
    "The Crocodile and the Monkey" ("Buaya and Beruk")
    "Pak Dungu" ("Mr. Stupid")
    "How Rice Came to Earth (1, 2)" ("The Origin of Rice")
    "The Widow and the Fishes"
Melalatoa, M. J. "Aman Jempret." In *Indonesian Folk Tales.* State Publishing and Printing House, Djakarta: Balai Pustaka, 1981.
    "An Honest Man" ("Aman Jempret")
Pratomo, Suyadi, narrator, and David T. Hill, translator. *Folk Tales from Irian Jaya.* Djakarta: P. N. Balai Pustaka, 1983.
    "The Sago Palm" ("The Origin of the Sago Palm: A Story from Mimika")
    "The Magic Crocodile" ("Watuwe, the Magic Crocodile: A Story from Arso")
Rassers, Dr. W. H. *Panji, the Culture Hero: A Structural Study of Religion in Java.* The Hague: Martinus Nijhoff, 1959.
    "The Legendary Jaka Tarub"
Soebiantoro, Afwani, and Manel Ratnatunga. *Folk Tales of Indonesia.* New Delhi: Sterling Publishers Pvt. Ltd., 1977.
    "The Overflowing Pot" ("The Disobedient Girl")
    "Kerta's Sin" ("Nyai Roro Kidul—Goddess of the South Sea")
    "Tiung Wanara" ("The Birth of Majapahit")
    "The Story of Sangkuriang"
    "A Toraja Tale" ("Toroja")
    "The Buffalo Wins!" ("Minangkabau")
Tjerita Rakjat 2. Djakarta: P. N. Balai Pustaka, 1963.
    "Ringkitan and the Cuscus" ("Si Ringkitan dan Kusoi")
Tjerita Rakjat 3. Djakarta: P. N. Balai Pustaka, 1963.
    "Pak Dungu"
    "Buaya and Beruk"
Usman, Zuber. *Tales from Indonesian Folklore* (Original title: *Dua Puluh Dongeng Anak-anak).* Translated from the Indonesian by Gary Lichtenstein. Djakarta: P. N. Balai Pustaka, 1982.
    "The Overflowing Pot" ("The Girl Who Wouldn't Follow Orders")
    "The Story of Sangkuriang" ("How Mount Tangkuban Perahu Came to Be")
    "A Toraja Tale" ("Story from Toraja Land")

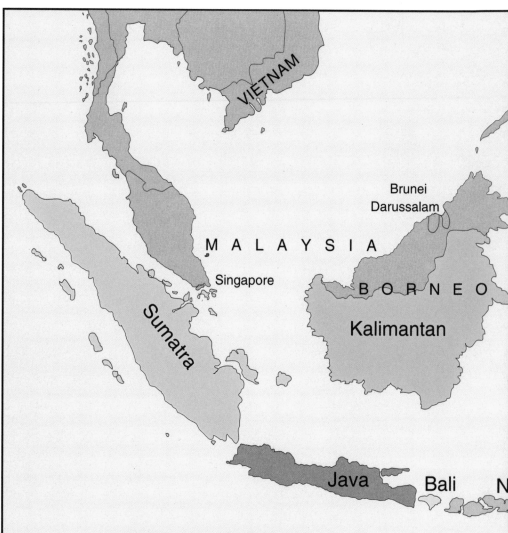

VIETNAM

Brunei
Darussalam

M A L A Y S I A

Singapore

B O R N E O

Sumatra

Kalimantan

Java   Bali   N

INDIAN OCEAN

INDONESIA

Adapted from a map by Marcia Bakry